The Patron Stone

By: Don McEnery

Edited by: Eileen Troemel
Cover Design: Natasha Williams of Dazed Designs
Copyright August 2023

Chapter 1 – Danger

The last few beams of light from the setting sun shone between the abandoned buildings of the Old Quarter of town. As Anise walked down the street, she patted down the corset of her full-length dress, stopping at her right hip where the dress flared out. Inside the pocket, she accessed her dagger.

"Dagger in place," she whispered before continuing. "One, two, three, four packets pinned into my dress. That should last a few nights."

In the twilight, ladies were already standing on many of the street corners. Anise approached one. "Victoria, how is your evening?"

"I use the name Vixen out here," she replied. "No men yet. It's payday for most factories though. Once the workers have paid their room and board they'll be headed for us."

Anise flashed a sinister smile. "They always want to have some fun with their pay."

"You're going to get caught one of these days," Vixen replied. "Not many people know what you do, but someday trouble will find you."

Anise smirked. "Anyone that deserves targeting?"

Vixen patted down her emerald dress. "Last week there were a few undesirable experiences. Classy and I both had a rough payday."

"Classy?" Anise asked.

"Cassandra," Vixen replied. "Pet names of a sort. If we ever elevate ourselves above this life our real names won't be stained."

"Just your bedsheets and souls," Anise remarked in disgust.

"A girl must eat," Vixen said. "We don't all have your talents."

Anise nodded. "The drug is useful. Beasts who abuse ladies in your profession deserve the punishment I inflict."

Vixen opened her palm and extended it slightly beyond her dress. "Do you have my coin?" she asked. "I give you deserving men, you give me a finder's fee. It's a good system."

Anise smiled. She handed Vixen a small coin purse. "Last week was a good haul. These perverts working in factories have tin chits and brass guineas; not just a pile of copper pennies like farmhands."

Vixen sighed as she tucked the purse inside her dress. "Factory workers are rougher than farmhands. They pay better, but is the money worth the soreness?"

Anise looked at a few nearby corners. "Have you seen Cassandra? I have her finder's fee purse from last week too."

"I saw a man approach her a short time ago," Vixen replied. "Depending on his interest she could be back any time, or we may not see her until tomorrow."

Whistles sounded in the distance.

"Factory shift end," Anise commented. "These streets will soon flood with your customers."

Vixen bit her bottom lip. "This is the part I dread."

"Pardon me?"

"The anticipation; will whoever takes me tonight be generous and gentle, or thrifty and barbarous?"

Anise inhaled deeply and shuddered as she exhaled. "I hate that feeling. Will my drug work well? Will he drink enough to pass out easily? I take the rough ones to avenge you and the others. If my tricks fail, I know it'll be a hard night."

"We all take risks," Vixen agreed. "I cannot imagine the reaction if one of those animals were to see you tamper with his drink."

"That's the largest single risk," Anise said. "I don't even remember who showed me what to mix. The memory is hazy. Regardless, I stand by my decision. Those who mistreat poor women, barely managing to live, deserve to be parted from their purse." Anise smiled while tapping her dress where the dagger was hidden. "They're lucky I don't part them from anything else."

Vixen gasped. "You wouldn't. You couldn't. Imagine the mess you'd be cleaning up."

They both laughed. Heads turned and eyes were focused on them from all directions. With smiles Anise and Vixen ran their fingers through their hair and tried to appear playful. Men from the factories headed down the street. The ladies standing, waiting, prepared their hair, arranged their dresses, and steadied themselves for the evening ahead.

Men invited women into inns and empty houses. Anise and Vixen exchanged glances. Vixen focused on one man in particular. "That one," she glanced and nodded. "That one deserves your treatment."

Anise nodded. "I should wait until he ventures this far down the street. Discretion is important for my work."

They observed as the man walked the street. Corner after corner he looked women up and down but continued forward.

Another man came to where Vixen and Anise were standing. "Are you ladies available tonight?"

"I am," Vixen replied. "I believe I see one of my friend's regular patrons a short distance away."

"I'm pleased to hear that," the man said. "I know a quiet little place we can go."

Vixen forced a kind smile and followed the man down the road. After a few blocks, they turned the corner.

The targeted man approached. He paused and eyed Anise up and down. His lips shifted but no sound came.

"Can I be of service this evening, Sir?" Anise asked.

"I'm certain you could try," he said. "I have what some would call exotic tastes."

"Exotic? Like ladies from other lands?" Anise inquired.

"Unconventional activity," he replied. "I like a lady who appears to be sturdy."

"I'm willing to try," Anise offered. "Should we get a few drinks and discuss my price?"

He nodded in agreement and Anise led him to a tavern. They walked down the cobblestone street with no discussion. Few of the pairings of the evening conversed in the street. The only sound was the combination of constant clicking and clacking of shoes on the stones.

They entered the tavern. The man went and sat at a table. He waved his arm motioning for Anise to head to the bar and fetch the drinks.

With her back to the man, Anise fished a coin purse out of her dress and a folded paper packet. She brought her hands together and tucked the paper into the cuff of her sleeve. She stood at the bar a moment before being served. "One stein of ale, and a glass of wine, please."

"Five copper if you have it," the bartender replied. "I'll take tin, but running low on copper."

Anise checked her purse. She smirked. "I can see four copper in here. If you're interested in small coins, maybe..."

"If you have a chit I'll take that," the bartender said, his face twisted. "I'm not losing money for a whore's smile."

Anise let out a quiet playful giggle and handed him the coin. "Here you go."

The bartender took the coin. He bit it, then shoved it into a pouch in his apron. He pulled a stein from the shelf and drew ale from the barrel behind him. He set the ale in front of Anise and turned to fetch a bottle of wine. While the bartender filled a wine glass Anise shook her wrist ever so slightly and powder from the paper in her sleeve descended into the stein.

"Your drinks," he announced as he set the wine beside the ale. "Enjoy."

Thank you," Anise said before taking the drinks back to the table.

She placed the stein in front of the man. "Your ale, Sir." She sat beside him and sipped her wine. "What are you looking for this evening?"

He drank a large gulp of the ale, set down the stein, and glared at Anise. "I'll tell you what I want as I want it. I expect no questions and complete obedience."

"How do I know what to charge?" Anise asked.

One side of his mouth raised into a half-smile. His cheek and eyebrow lifted along with his lip. "I'll be your only client tonight. Just charge me based on that."

Anise listed his demands like a vendor itemizing a purchase order. "Whole night? Mystery activities, and a declaration that you want total obedience? Anything else?"

He gulped down the remaining ale. "Another drink."

Anise nodded in compliance. She drank some of the wine and took both glasses up to the bar.

She returned with her glass and his stein refilled. "Here you are."

He didn't speak. He simply chugged the ale and demanded another.

Again, Anise drank a small portion of her wine and took both drinks to be refilled.

"Why do you take your drink each time?" the man asked. "It's not empty."

Quickly Anise replied with a fake giggle. "I take both so I make fewer trips and we have more time together."

He grunted and kept drinking. Anise sipped her wine and stared at him intently. Occasionally she flashed a smile. He ignored her and focused on the drink.

"I've thought about my rate for tonight," Anise said. "Given your requests, I'd like to charge a bronze guinea."

He spat out a mouthful of ale. Many patrons of the tavern looked over. The man flashed an angered stare and people returned to their drinks. "That's twenty-five copper pennies," he hissed. "No whore is worth that. Most men don't make that much in a fortnight."

"You say most men," Anise smiled. "You're not most men. I can tell. There's something special about you. And I'm not just some average whore. I promise you a night you'll never forget."

He stared at her.

"You've also had two tin chits worth of ale. I need my purse refilled for that in addition to my services."

He stared at her again. "Fifteen copper is a lot. You're not going to see that from any farmhand looking to spend the night."

Anise smiled. "You're not a farmhand. And you request more than they do."

He nodded. "Not backing down. I respect that. Another ale or two and I'll agree to your terms."

Anise nodded in agreement. The man finished his drink and Anise made another trip to the bar. She slipped another packet of powder into the man's drink while the barkeep's back was turned. Again, the man finished the stein in a single mouthful. Anise sipped her wine.

The man looked at his empty mug. "No more to drink. It's getting, getting late. We should find a room."

"There are empty houses a few streets away. We can surely find somewhere unoccupied that has a bed." Anise stood up and took the man's hand. They left the empty stein and half-empty wine glass on the table and walked out.

Anise led the man down the road. She popped her head inside several empty houses. The man staggered and stumbled in tow.

"We need to find shomewhere shoon," he slurred. "That ale's stronger than I thought."

"We should be somewhere suitable very soon," Anise assured him as she popped into another house and backed out. "Some of these abandoned houses have foul smells or broken beds. We want somewhere good."

"Every time we... we reject a house," he slurred, "I'm getting less, and less, and less, for my coin. Find shomewhere shoon or I'll walk away and not pay you anything."

Anise looked away down the street and started blinking. "Stalling time is over," she whispered to herself.

"What'sh over?" he demanded.

"Our search," Anise replied quickly. "This house should be suitable."

They walked in. There was wood, a bed, and nobody in the house. No food or dishes.

"Vacant house," Anise announced. "I'll get a small fire started to keep us warm."

Anise scrambled together some kindling and a few split logs while the man stumbled his way to the bed. He removed his shoes and sat on the bed.

"Hu-hurry with that fire," the man demanded.

Anise approached the bed. She began loosening her clothing. She reached forward and started opening the man's shirt. She went methodically, button by button, teasing him.

He grabbed her by the shoulders and spun her onto the bed. "Let's not way-sh-te any, any more time."

He tore his shirt off and mounted Anise. He grasped her hair and started hissing at her neck.

Anise made some moaning noises of pleasure. "Mmm, how shall we begin?"

There was no answer.

"Sir?"

Silence.

His eyes were closed. Anise squirmed out from under him. He didn't react. She straightened and rearranged her clothing. No reaction. She covered the man with a blanket and removed his pants. The man began to snore. She patted him down and searched his clothing. She found three small coin purses; she moved them up and down in her hand and smiled at the weight. Anise quickly tucked the purses into her dress. She added a couple of logs to the fire and scurried out of the house.

Anise headed down the street. Most of the ladies were gone from the street corners. She kept walking down the street. "Time to get some sleep."

Chapter 2 – Awakening

"What am I laying on?" Anise moaned feeling around. With a hiss, she pulled her finger from the surface and looked at her hand. "A splinter?" No mattress lay beneath her, only rough wood.

Was, was I drugged? she thought to herself. *No, my head's too clear to be waking up from drug or drink.*

She stood turning and analyzing the room while she collected her thoughts. *Stone wall, opening with no glass, just bars, looks old.* She continued her assessment, cataloguing her surroundings. *Bricks, wood door, iron hinges. That looks newer.* The contents of the room puzzled her. *Shipping crates, barrels. Am I at the docks? Is this a storehouse?* She closed her eyes, inhaled, and listened. *There's no smell of seawater, no sounds of merchants, stale air, could it be a warehouse? Am I still in the Old Quarter?* She heard voices and noises outside the little room. She ran her hands through her hair. Her mind raced, *who's there? What's going on?* She cautiously inched closer to the door. She leaned toward it to listen. The voices were impossible to discern. *Who has me?*

Her breathing quickened. She spun around faster, looking for some opening other than the door. She started patting her dress; she slowed as she passed over her right shin.

She felt around and whispered, "My dagger. Whoever put me here mustn't have searched me."

As she caressed the dagger handle, her breathing began to calm. She drew the blade from its scabbard. The wavy kris dagger reflected the light coming through the small window. She went to the walls and started feeling them and tapping at the mortar between the bricks. Her hands recoiled from the touch of the cold stone. The clinking and clacking of the dagger echoed through the little room. Anise heard the voices getting louder and closer. She whirled around frantically, breathing quickly again, looking for anything to use when her captors opened the door. After three revolutions she stopped and looked down with dismay. She saw her hand and realized she was holding her dagger. As the voices drew near, she moved to the side of the room, behind the door. She lifted the dagger shoulder high, ready to plunge it into whoever entered the room. The few moments waiting felt like an eternity. Her chest heaved from deep breaths, sweat trickled down her face, and the dagger in her raised arm seemed to weigh more and more with each breath. She wiped her forehead and waited.

With a creak, the door opened. A tall bald man walked in. As soon as he was past the edge of the open door Anise lunged forward with her dagger plunging it into the man's left shoulder.

"I really wish people wouldn't do that," the man snarled. He turned and glared into Anise's eyes. His stare froze her; it was furious and commanding. "Sit," he barked pointing at the shipping crate she woke up on.

Anise watched as the man reached over his shoulder and pulled the dagger out. Anise gasped; the fluid oozing from the wound was thick and purple. "W–who are you?"

"Thraz," he replied with less of a snarl. He raised his hand to his shoulder. The hand became sheathed in a green glow. He waved it over the wound. Slowly, the wound closed. "Sit," he repeated, pointing with the dagger.

Anise cautiously crept over and sat down. "What are you?" she asked trembling. "Am I hallucinating? Is this an opium den?" she continued frantically, almost seeming to be addressing herself. She looked back at Thraz, "Why am I here? What do you want with me?"

Thraz handed Anise her dagger. "You're here because you've been awakened."

"Awakened?" she questioned.

"I'm a demon," Thraz started. "You're part demon. All those stories about Heaven and Hell, angels and demons, they're true, part true. There's a war going on. Anise Lovejoy, you've been conscripted."

Anise gasped. "How do you know my name?"

"The Clairvoyant," Thraz replied.

"Clairvoyant?" Anise echoed. She gripped the dagger handle tighter. She looked at her dagger; there was a syrupy purple liquid on the blade. She looked up at Thraz. The same purple liquid oozed down his arm. His face was plain, no signs of pain or discomfort.

"She senses demonic auras and we summon them," Thraz said.

Anise planted her feet on the floor, trembling and shuddering, barely able to sit straight. Thraz let out a huff and looked back toward the door. As soon as he looked away Anise sprang up and sprinted for the door, slashing Thraz across the belly as she passed. He grunted but made no move to block her escape.

When Anise entered the next room she was paralyzed by what she saw. Demons were real. She saw men and women, some human looking some not, with various types of weapons sparring and attacking dummies. Off to one side, she saw tables and chairs with people sitting and someone standing; a lecture of some sort. She returned her focus to the armed group. She saw glowing manifestations of weapons in their hands. Some were orange, some purple, a couple blue, a few yellow, and one was the same green glow as Thraz's hand when he closed the wound on his shoulder.

Wide-eyed, Anise whispered, "how can this be real?"

"It just is," Thraz replied casually. "Now we need to find out what kind of demon you are."

"Kind of demon?" Anise blurted out. "There are kinds?"

"Yes," Thraz answered. "Those colours you see around their weapons are an indication of their heritage. It's their use of DHEC."

"Deck? Like on a ship?"

"An acronym," Thraz chuckled. "Demonic Heritage Energy Channel, or DHEC for short, is how we wield the power of our ancestors."

Anise continued to scan the room. There were so many peculiar sights and so much new information. Her eyes continued to wander in bewilderment. "What am I then? And how do I use this DHEC?"

Thraz pulled a grey egg-shaped stone from a pouch on his belt. "We can discover your heritage with this crystal; it shows us our true selves."

"Crystal," Anise scoffed. "I've seen a lot of gems and jewelry and that's a pretty plain-looking rock."

Thraz scowled. His eyes narrowed and he stared into Anise's eyes; like before but deeper, harder.

Anise began to tremble. "It's like you're staring into my soul." She gulped and coughed, choking on her breath.

"The crystal glows when DHEC energy is channelled into it," Thraz finally said. He grasped the stone, closed his eyes, and made a humming sound. The crystal began to glow green. "The green shows that I'm a reaper demon; a demon of life and death energy."

"I've been a thief using deceit and drugs to rob men for years," Anise blurted out. She stopped. She covered her mouth and her face became stricken with terror. "Forget I said that."

"We know your past," Thraz said. "Seducing young men, taking them wherever you could, disguised as a prostitute, and then drugging them so you could take their belongings and give nothing in return."

Anise's face paled. Her eyes widened, her whole body began shaking, and her lips trembled. Taking a few deep breaths, she managed to centre herself and suppress the trembling. "How does the crystal work?"

"Hold it and concentrate on your life, your past, your secrets, and the crystal will know."

"How?" Anise asked.

"Just do it," Thraz barked.

"I don't understand," she protested. "You've brought me to this building, pulled my dagger out of your arm and the blood was purple, shown me a room of unimaginable sights, you're telling me I'm a demon, and now you expect me to use some magic rock?" With each item she listed her voice became more strained. Her eyes welled up with tears.

"You were born for this," Thraz replied. "You just need to concentrate."

Anise took the crystal. She took a few breaths and tried to calm herself. She clasped it in her hands and closed her eyes. She began to think about her childhood. Images appeared above her hands.

Anise gasped. "Is the crystal producing these images?"

Thraz nodded. "It is. Focus your thoughts."

Anise saw scenes of herself as a young girl growing up on the streets. There were vivid images of street walkers selling their bodies for money, many of whom were battered with no spark of life left in their eyes. She scowled with resentment at images of the monsters disguised as men who would do such a deed. Then, there was a hazy memory of a figure who taught her about opium and other drugs. Her thoughts shifted to her adult life; powders, a mortar and pestle, no faces, seducing men to rob them.

As she concentrated, she felt a warmth in her hands. The crystal radiated a welcoming heat. She opened her eyes and hands. The once grey stone was now a vibrant lilac. Anise dropped the crystal. It bounced on the floor and rolled returning to its original grey.

"Purple," Thraz observed as he walked over and picked the crystal from the floor. "I should have known a seductress would have a succubus lineage."

Anise couldn't believe her ears. "Succubus?"

"Demons who seduce and trick," Thraz said. "Somewhere in your ancestry, there was a union and a part demon child. Now you're the offspring. There's a war starting, and I need you to cooperate." Thraz's teeth gritted. Each word sounded harsher than the last.

Anise stood frozen, a blank stare in her eyes. Her focus wandered the room in disbelief. The images before her were undeniably there clear as day, but somehow also a hazy collection of indistinguishable images. The paralysis broke when she heard a voice.

"You're new here."

"Ye, yes," Anise stuttered.

The man approaching her wore an ancient soldier's metal armour and carried a spear. He had wild red hair and appeared to be in his early twenties. He stopped a few steps short of Anise. "I'm Garrett."

"Garrett here is a fury," Thraz said. "Descended of a fallen angel. He's assigned as your trainer, partner, and protector."

Anise stared blankly. "Trainer? Partner?"

Garrett stepped forward. "We hunt in pairs or small groups. When someone new comes in an experienced Infernal serves as a mentor."

"In-Infernal?" Anise struggled to even say the word.

"It's what we call ourselves as part demon," Garrett explained. "Let Thraz check on the other chambers. We should start."

Thraz handed Anise a necklace before he left. It was a black metal chain with a black stone pendant, a simple round stone. Once Anise took hold of the pendant it morphed into a set of bat's wings folded in.

"What's this?" Anise asked.

"Just put it on," Thraz growled, walking away. "You'll figure it out."

Garrett chuckled. "Come with me, Anise. I'll get you started."

"How do you know my name?" Anise asked

"Thraz told me your name when he gave me this assignment," Garrett replied.

They walked to a corner of the room with a few crates. Garrett sat down and gestured for Anise to join him.

"Let's see your weapon," Garrett ordered. His tone was much more serious than before. Something about his eyes changed as well. From friendly and light-hearted, to serious business.

Anise lifted her dagger. "Here."

"Watch me," Garrett instructed. He took his spear in both hands and closed his eyes. He made a humming noise and a tremor ran through his body. Suddenly he began to change. He got taller, sprouted wings with black feathers, and his skin tone was altered by an orange hue. "This is my true form."

"True form?" Anise could barely get the words out. "How did you do that?"

"DHEC," Garrett replied. "I harness it, channel it, and bend it to my will."

Anise was silent for a moment. Her eyes widened and then narrowed. "So I'm conscripted into this demon war, does that mean I need to go hunt angels? Or do I get to go after God?" she said sarcastically.

"The Touched," Garrett answered abruptly. "They were created to serve, but they became corrupted."

"So, why would a demon care about corruption?" Anise asked. "Don't you live for that?"

"Not their kind," Garrett said. "I'll have time to explain that later. For now, you need to focus."

Anise took a deep breath. "Focus on what?"

"Your DHEC control," Garrett snapped. "I didn't show you that transformation to brag."

Anise took hold of the necklace. "With this I suppose?"

Garrett simply nodded. He reached into his armour and pulled out a necklace of his own. The pendant had feathered wings fully outstretched. "When yours looks like this, you'll be ready."

Anise clasped her pendant in her hands. She felt a mild pulsating sensation. "It's throbbing, what do I do?"

Garrett raised his hand to silence her. "Focus, just focus."

Anise closed her eyes and thought about everything she had seen since she woke up. She held the stone. The pulse was irregular. Intensifying, it caused Anise's hands to jerk around. Her hold on the stone loosened; it jumped from her hands and bounced off her chest.

Garrett looked Anise in the eyes. He produced a kind smile. "Remove doubt. This is all new, but you must believe us, you belong here."

Anise held the pendant tight and moved her hands to her chest. "This is a part of me," she said with an attempt at conviction. Anise's body responded to the pendant through a series of twitches and spasms. The stone's pulse quickened and so did Anise's. Each time the stone's pulse sped up, Anise's tried to catch it; one would slow and so would the other.

Anise thought about the words she had heard: demon, succubus, DHEC, transformation, true form, Infernal. She mouthed the words, repeated them randomly, and then began whispering her thoughts. The noises of the room faded. The clanging of the metal weapons, breaking of wooden boards, shouts and screams, the conversations, they all silenced. The pendant pulse and Anise's pulse synchronized. Finally, everything was about this necklace, these thoughts, and this strange sensation emanating from the pendant.

"Infernal, succubus, true form, demon, succubus, DHEC, demon, succubus, Infernal, transformation, true form, demon, Lilith." Anise stopped. "Lilith," she repeated looking at Garrett, "who is Lilith?"

"Succubus queen," Garrett answered with concern in his voice. "How would you know about Lilith?"

"I don't know. I've never heard that name before." Anise looked at her hands. "The wings, they've started to open."

Garrett looked. "You've tapped into something. We should see what you can channel."

Anise closed her eyes again. "Channel, channel." She gripped the pendant tightly and her hands began to shake. "Succubus, Infernal, DHEC, channel, Lilith, Infernal." As she spoke her eyelids fluttered. Her head bobbed back and forth. Her hands trembled; the tremor extended to her arms, then her chest, and finally to her entire body. Her entire body convulsed violently as she continued repeating words. A purple aura began to emanate from her hands. It swelled and engulfed her entire body.

Garrett's eyes widened and Thraz rushed over. "what did she do?" Thraz asked.

Garrett's bewilderment almost prevented him from speaking. "She chanted words, held her pendant, and said Lilith's name. She's trying to channel more power now and this shaking started."

Thraz grabbed both of Garrett's shoulders and looked him deep in the eyes. "This isn't just shaking, this is serious! Her demonic aura is almost as strong as mine, and I'm a full-blooded demon."

Garrett's jaw dropped. His stunned silence spoke more than words could. All this time Anise was clutching her pendant and chanting. The aura glowed brighter and pulsed as it expanded away from her. Most of the other Infernals in the room stopped their activities to observe the spectacle.

Garrett shook his head and returned to his senses. "How do we stop her?"

"We can't," Thraz replied. "We have to let this conclude naturally. Everyone take cover!"

As Thraz bellowed out the order every Infernal in the room stopped and looked around. Most of them ran around or jumped behind shipping crates, a few hid behind the iron columns inside, a few even left the building.

"Lilith, Lilith, hear me." Anise stopped the chanting, her words became a prayer. "Lilith, Queen of the Succubi, hear my plea. Grant me the power, the strength, the ability, to fight this war. Bestow upon thine humble servant the gifts you are capable of. Lilith, hear me. I beseech thee."

Suddenly, Anise collapsed on the floor. The aura faded and disappeared. Thraz and Garrett approached slowly. Garrett knelt down and examined her. "She breathes. She's alive!" He picked her up and cradled her motionless body as he carried her back to the small room and placed her on the shipping crate.

When Anise regained consciousness, she turned her head to see Garrett sitting on a barrel beside her. He was slumped forward with his eyes closed. "What happened?"

Garrett raised and shook his head. "You chanted and went into some trance. You started praying to Lilith. Your demonic aura was huge. Then you collapsed. It's been about two days."

"Two days!" Anise exclaimed. "I was asleep for two days?"

"You were," Garrett replied. "Your hands never moved from your pendant. They were seized around it."

"Pendant?" Anise slowly shifted as she looked around. "My pendant? Where?"

"Still around your neck," Garrett replied pointing.

Anise still had her hands clamped around the pendant as she sat up. She slowly opened her hands and looked inside. Anise gasped. She saw that not only had the wings opened like Garrett's pendant, but there were arms, legs, a head, a face, and even a whip in the right hand. "It's so...developed."

Garrett stared silently.

"Have you seen anything like this before?" Anise asked with wonder.

Garrett shook his head. "No, mine is the most developed of any pendant here. Was, I guess." He reached forward extending his fingers toward Anise's pendant.

"Stop," she recoiled as the word came out. Her hands encased the pendant once again. "I don't know why, but I don't want anyone else to touch it."

Puzzled, Garrett withdrew his hand. "I don't know why either. I never cared if anyone reached for my pendant."

Anise's fingers opened to make a flesh cage around the figure her pendant had become. "I want to chant again. I want to commune with my DHEC energy."

"Do you think that's wise?" Garrett asked nervously. "You were unconscious for two days. Maybe you should approach demonic energy slowly."

Anise shook her head. "Something is driving me to try again. An urge, beyond words, I can't explain it."

Garrett shook his head. "Thraz would know more than we do. Or he could summon another demon to this realm to help you."

Anise ignored his objection and chanted. "Lilith, succubus, DHEC, demon, Infernal, succubus, true form, Lilith, channel, channel." The purple aura began to glow around her. Her pupils dilated and her voice became raspy. "Li-li-th. He-ear me. Grant me st-rength. Grant me po-wer. Li-li-th." Uttering the syllables, her body convulsed. The aura emanating from her pulsated as it swelled. A smile came across her face.

"Lilith, I feel the power you grant me. I feel your strength becoming my own. I beseech you to channel more. I want to be stronger. Help me." The aura and her smile widened. With each word, her eyes began to glow with a purple light. She shuddered a few times and fell back to her crate, seated. Her hands released the pendant and she exhaled "uh, hu hu hu". Her head twitched slightly and a euphoric grin came to her mouth. She let out one more breath and fell sideways. She was unconscious.

Garrett shook his head. "This does not bode well for her."

Chapter 3 – Merging

nise groaned as she regained consciousness. Her hand covered part of her face and she shook trying but unable to sit up. "How long?"

Thraz and Garrett stood over the crate she slept on. "A few hours," Thraz replied.

Anise put her hand on her head. Her eyes winced. Sluggishly, she sat up. Her hand reached for her chest. "My pendant," she gasped, feeling around.

"We took it," Thraz told her. "You're not safe with it. We need to figure out why these reactions are happening."

"I need it," Anise blurted out. Her eyes darted back and forth examining the room. She scanned the boxes, the walls, Garrett and Thraz's, hands. "Where?" she demanded. "Return it!"

Thraz raised his hand to calm Anise. "I've sent my imp to bring a clairvoyant. They will be better able to understand this than we are."

"Until then?" Anise questioned.

"Wait," Garrett snapped. "You wait."

"I need to get stronger," Anise protested. "I need Lilith's strength inside me."

"You don't know what you're saying," Thraz argued.

"It's not about what I say," Anise tried to explain. "It's about what I feel. I feel the need to channel more power."

As they stared at each other, a woman entered the room. "I'm the clairvoyant, Aleesa. Where is the succubus?"

Anise stood. "I'm here. Anise."

Aleesa's piercing gaze settled on Thraz and Garrett. "Her amulet," she demanded with her arm thrust toward them.

Thraz took the necklace from his pocket and handed it to Aleesa. The instant Anise saw the pendant she lunged forward. "Mine!"

Garrett stepped between Anise and Aleesa to stop her. Anise stopped and crouched. She pulled the dagger from the sheath under her dress. "Get out of my way."

Garrett stood firm. He reached behind him and pulled a pointed rod from a holster on his back. He gave his arm a mild flick and the rod extended to become a spear. "Let Aleesa do her job. I can't allow you to interfere."

"You can't stop me," Anise insisted. "You mustn't try." She swung her arm from side to side slashing her dagger through the air. Garrett stood still as a statue. His eyes watched the blade; as it inched closer he watched more intently. Anise was feverish and sweating, but Garrett remained calm. As the dagger approached Garrett simply flicked his wrist. The side of his spear collided with Anise's dagger. There was a clang as metal hit metal and a clatter as the dagger hit the floor.

Anise screamed and threw herself at Garrett. Mid-lunge her aura began to glow, her fingers elongated into claws, and she extended her arm. Garrett began twirling his spear; producing an orange glow. Anise's aura collided with Garrett's and both were knocked back.

Garrett jumped to his feet stunned. "That's never happened before!"

"Stand firm," Thraz ordered. He drew a sickle from his belt. It began to glow green and the aura took the form of a scythe.

Anise picked herself up and stood facing Thraz. Garrett moved to Thraz's side. Anise howled and swiped the talons formed by her aura. She pressed forward. They blocked her attacks. The aura collisions made thunderous booming noises which attracted some of the other Infernals. As they peered into the room Thraz barked, "stay out!"

Anise continued to howl and thrash. A pair of large bat-like wings sprouted from her back, her skin changed to a shade of lavender, and horns sprouted from just below her hairline. Her hair colour changed to black. Thraz watched the transformation in awe. "It's a full transformation without the pendant. How?"

"Pay-tron st-one," Anise groaned between her screams of rage. "Li-li-th. St-one. Pow-wer." Groaning, she reached forward but Garrett batted her hand with the shaft of his spear.

"Stop!" shouted Aleesa. "Let her through. She may have her patron stone returned."

Garrett and Thraz stepped aside and allowed their auras to fade. Once they opened a path Anise scurried between them and grabbed the necklace from Aleesa's outstretched hand.

"She called it patron stone first," Garrett observed. "None of us used that term around her before. How did she know?"

Aleesa looked from Thraz to Garrett. "She's a royal. My visions show she is truly a daughter of Lilith herself. How she came to grow up in the mortal realm I cannot say."

Anise clutched the pendant to her chest. Her head and chest weaved from side to side. She wasn't chanting but her aura was glowing again. She didn't react to Aleesa's words.

"Did she even hear you?" Thraz asked. "What kind of a trance must she be in."

Aleesa reached an open palm toward Anise and closed her eyes. Alessa's eyelids fluttered for a moment. Her fingers clenched and reopened. She opened her eyes and spoke. "She's learning to commune with the DHEC. It's something new and familiar all at once. You should speak to her about it when she's ready."

Aleesa walked away leaving Thraz and Garrett with stunned expressions. Garrett looked at Thraz. "How do we know when she'll be ready?" he asked naively. "I've never seen this before."

Thraz sheathed his sickle. "I haven't either. I guess we wait for her to stop passing out every time she channels."

They watched Anise continue to shake and produce a stronger and stronger aura. Her chanting and prayer returned. "Li-li-th. Mah-th-ur. Grant stre-ength. Gr-ant pah-wah-er." Anise shuddered harder and her aura intensified with each syllable.

"We can't intervene," Thraz commented.

Garrett met Thraz's eyes. "If she unleashes all her new power, we can't stop her either."

Thraz nodded. "I know. If we had trouble when Aleesa had her patron stone, then no Infernal here is strong enough to manage fighting her, not with this power."

Full of concern, Garrett's eyes shifted from Anise to his spear and back. His grip tightened and loosened, unsure of what was to come.

After several minutes of chanting Anise finally said something new, "Pay-ter-on st-oh-ne. Com-p-lee-te me."

Anise fell silent. She opened the palms of her hands against her chest. There was an intense lilac light radiating from the openings between her fingers. She continued opening her palms and drawing her fingers closer to her chest. Finally, her hands lay flat with only the tips of her fingers touching. The stone was gone.

"What happened?" Garrett asked.

"I've merged with my patron stone," Anise replied. "I understand now."

"Understand what?" Thraz asked.

"I was born a demon, made a mortal, grew up in this realm, and now I've been reborn as my true self. I'm a Royal; a daughter of Lilith. Through the DHEC she told me her plan. I was created to be a soldier here, to protect the souls of the mortals from the Touched. It's still my job to seduce and corrupt, but Lilith has given me a higher cause. To keep them pure so they can die clean and become fuel for the armies of hell."

"You learned all that from DHEC?" Garrett exclaimed.

Anise simply stared at him. "The patron stone calls each of us. Our parents have set us on a path. When your bond is strong enough you too may merge with your patron stone. Only then will you have a true understanding."

Chapter 4 – Hunting

nise walked down the street. She paused, feigning adjustments to her clothing. Her adjustments, coupled with the sounds of the street, helped hide Anise observing her surroundings. She noted the lamplighter made his rounds, setting his flame to the lamps along the road. The workday was done. With the dinner hour nearly finished, and the sun setting, Anise's work would soon begin. Workers occupied the portion of the Old Quarter closest to town. Heading away from town, Anise saw more desolate and abandoned homes. Her pace slowed as she transitioned from the residential area to her hunting ground.

A voice broke the silence. "Getting ready for the hunt?"

Anise spun around. "Garrett, I told you not to do that!"

Garrett smiled. "Sorry, I like to keep you alert. The Touched can be anywhere, anyone."

Anise shook her head. "Keep your eyes out for the new Infernal. Our orders are to bring him in tonight."

"I miss the summoning method," Garrett lamented. "That's how we got to the clutch. Someday we'll be a full-fledged legion."

"It's become too dangerous," Anise replied. "The summoning trance renders you helpless. It's safer if we retrieve our new initiates."

Garrett sighed. "I know. I'd rather be out hunting the Touched than babysitting more initiates."

Anise smirked. "Last one give you too much trouble?"

Garrett glared at her. "That possession thing you did, and merging with your patron stone had us very worried."

Walking down the street, they checked the alleyways and gaps between buildings. The click-clack of their shoes on the cobblestone sidewalk made the only sound to break the silence of the night. Every so often Garrett would stop and move his head, to listen for any other being.

After a few stops, Anise broke the silence. "I agree; we should be hunting. We're the top pair in the clutch. This new Infernal must be a pretty high priority for Thraz to have assigned us to a retrieval mission."

Garrett's head jerked and looked down an alleyway. "Did you hear that?"

Anise stopped and listened. There was a scraping noise; something was being dragged across the stone. "Scraping. Could be a Touched."

Humming, she and Garrett drew their weapons. Anise's kris knife glowed purple, emerging from beneath her dress. Garrett's spear glimmered orange.

Stealthily, Garrett entered the alley in front of Anise. He pointed his spear forward as they crept down the narrow space. His eyes constantly scanned side to side.

"Who goes there?" Garrett called out.

The scraping continued, followed by a long groan, and then a second. Anise moved her dagger to her left hand. She flicked out her right arm and her demonic aura formed a crackling purple whip. "At least two bodies moving, probably Shamblers."

"You catch, and I'll dispatch," Garrett chuckled.

Anise's aura whip crackled as the energy flowed through it. Purple sparks flickered into the air. Through the flickering light, two large lumbering silhouettes appeared at the end of the alley. They were large, at least a foot taller than an average man, and wider in the upper body. As Garrett and Anise approached, the light radiating from their weapons provided enough light to see the grey skin tone of the creatures. Garrett aimed his spear at the Shambler on the left. The two figures shuffled forward.

"Hunters," one of them groaned.

The other tilted its head toward the first. "Reward for their bodies, dead or alive."

The first stopped and looked at the second. "We should turn. Their power make strong Shambler."

"No," the second protested. "Easier to kill and bring bodies to lair."

The Shamblers faced each other, squaring off. Both of their chests heaved with deep breaths. Each exhaled through the nose into the other's face. Their eyes locked and their fists clenched then flung open exposing their claws. Anise and Garrett advanced without a reaction from the creatures. The Shamblers bent their knees, raising their arms and pulling their clawed hands up beside their faces.

Before either could lunge forward, Anise lashed her whip around the neck of the first. "We don't have time for this," she groaned.

Garrett charged forward and thrust the glowing tip of his spear through the neck of the other one. "No more groaning from that one," he said pulling the spear out. The creature crumpled to the ground.

The second Shambler roared, flailing its claws toward Garrett. Anise tugged on her whip; hauling the creature to the ground. Garrett plunged his spear into the heart of the Shambler. It let out a cry before its eyes rolled back in their sockets and its body went limp on the ground.

"Thankfully aura weapons dispatch these abominations quickly," Anise observed.

"I wonder why," Garrett said. "They were made by the forces of the other realm to fight angels and demons. Why wouldn't their creators include a resistance to demonic energy?"

Anise allowed her aura whip to disappear and sheathed her dagger. "I don't know. It does seem odd."

Garrett shook his spear and the orange glow faded as it retracted down to its smaller size before he sheathed it. "Alright, check these bodies quickly and then we can find the initiate."

"Check them for what?"

"Glyphs, talismans, angelic or demonic symbols, anything we can use," Garrett replied kneeling down. Anise knelt beside the other Shambler. They scoured the bodies from head to toe, rifling through pockets, removing shoes, even checking hair.

"Nothing here but tattered clothing," Anise said. "All the pockets are empty. No bag or purse."

"Not a thing on mine either," Garrett grumbled, thumping his fist on the body. "At least we got to do some hunting. Let's go find that Infernal."

"Wait," Anise said. "What about the bodies? We can't leave them for regular people to find?"

"They'll be fine," Garrett replied as he walked. "There's enough sickness going around with these new factories, all this smoke from the coal, they'll be assumed sick from exposure."

Anise looked at him. "Even if they weren't abnormally large, and their skin wasn't almost grey, there are holes from your aura spear in one's neck and the other's chest. It'll become a murder investigation. Coal smoke and epidemics can't explain that."

Garrett stomped back. "We can do the release. Get your glyph torch out."

Anise reached under her dress and pulled out a small metal rod. The end glowed. "Here."

"Draw the release glyph on them," Garrett commanded impatiently.

Anise scrambled to make the proper marking with the glowing end of the rod. First, she drew a semicircular arch and a line closing it, the shape of a door. Next, she made an X across the door. As she finished, the glyph flashed with red sparks. The body slowly dissolved into thin air. Anise repeated the process on the second Shambler.

Garrett paced, watching the bodies crumble and fade away to nothing. "Now, let's find our initiate." He walked faster than before. Every corner and alleyway he paused and looked, then hurried to the next. With her dress on it was difficult for Anise to keep pace with Garrett's stride and speed; by the time he had gone down three blocks, she had only managed two.

"Stop," Anise called. "Come back."

Garrett stomped back to Anise. "If you can't hunt in that dress why don't you wear something that gives you better mobility?"

Anise had her hand on her chest. "My stone, it reacted to something. I think we're close."

"Sorry," Garrett muttered. "This mission is annoying me."

"I understand," Anise replied. "I wear the dress to blend in. Look at these streets; women wear dresses here. Only the men wear pants."

"And when you act as bait for the Touched using illusions you need to blend in," Garrett commented, nodding his head.

"Exactly," Anise said. "Hiding in plain sight. The illusion glyph you use just keeps that ancient armour looking like modern clothing, but it only fools the regular humans."

There was a clicking noise. Someone was walking on the stones of the alleyway. Garrett drew his spear again and stepped in front of Anise. They crept into the alleyway. In front of them, a man with a pot belly and grey hair with a touch of white wandered with no sense of purpose.

"Sir," Garrett called out. "Are you alright?" The old man didn't answer. He didn't stumble or shuffle about like a drunk. He just paced with no visible reaction to Garrett's words.

"Excuse me, sir," Anise called. "Are you alright?" The man continued pacing with no indication that he heard Anise.

"He's either our initiate or some Touched setting a trap," Garrett said. He raised his spear handle and extended his weapon to full length.

Anise fluttered her eyelids. She hummed for a moment. Her right palm began to glow purple and her aura whip crackled as it manifested. They crept toward the man cautiously, surveying the alley for any other figures. As they reached the man he mumbled something unintelligible and collapsed. Garrett knelt beside the body and put his hand on the man's head. "I can sense a demonic aura. We need to get him to Thraz."

Garrett put his spear away and hoisted the man onto his shoulders. "Let's move quickly."

Anise nodded and dismissed her aura whip. They hurried through the town streets and headed for the warehouse in the Old Quarter. It was late enough that most people, even those partaking in evening entertainment, were off the streets. Anise and Garrett arrived at the warehouse without incident.

Chapter 5 – Quickening

They burst through the door Garrett called, "Thraz! We found the Infernal, but he needs help."

Thraz rushed over. "Get him to one of the small rooms." Garrett nodded. While Garrett carried the initiate, Thraz turned to Anise. "What happened?"

"We don't know," Anise replied. "He was wandering in an alley. He didn't respond to us. As we approached, he collapsed. We sensed his aura, so we brought him in."

Silently, Thraz marched to the small storage room. Moments later, Garrett walked out and closed the door.

Anise hurried to Garrett. He met her eyes with a long face. "Thraz is trying to channel some healing energy. He's not certain what affliction the man has."

Anise stared at Garrett. A tear came to her eye. "We almost missed him."

Garrett sighed heavily. "You're right. We almost did...because of my impatience." Garrett growled. He stormed over to a group of weapon training dummies and started angrily jabbing them with his spear. Anise watched as Garrett transitioned from lightly jabbing, to lunging in, to using his demonic aura with the spear. He used the aura spear like a staff, bludgeoning the training dummy until it was a pile of rubble on the floor.

Garrett destroying the dummy caught the attention of the Infernals in the room. Muttering from them became a steady thrum under the sounds of Garrett brutalizing the dummy. Whispered phrases came through the overall drone.

"That's one of our leaders?" an Infernal questioned.

"Such a temper; he's little more than a child," another scoffed.

"So much strength wasted on someone who can't control his emotions," someone said sarcastically.

With each set of words, Garrett's facial expressions changed. His eyes narrowed, his lips quivered, and his head switched from side to side looking for the mouth that uttered the offending words. Sweat streamed down his face. He huffed, harder and harder. Finally, Garrett put his spear away and stormed out of the warehouse.

Anise surveyed the faces in the room and scowled. There were stunned and guilty expressions among the lot. She stared into the eyes of every Infernal there. Words were not needed. After only eye contact, many of the Infernals hung their heads in shame. Anise dashed out the door after Garrett.

The streetlights glowed, but the darkness of the night swallowed the light making it difficult to see. Anise put her hand to her chest where her patron stone had merged with her. She channelled the DHEC energy, seeking ripples in the flow which might lead her to Garrett.

Anise walked the nearby streets. Her gaze rested on the decrepit buildings, she muttered. "The Old Quarter has a lot of abandoned buildings. Most people left when the factories came and the docks were built." She passed the stone and wood houses and saw broken windows and half-open doors. She drew her dagger and clenched her hand around it. The colour faded from her fingers. Her eyes darted from side to side, not sure where to focus.

She walked the streets listening for any noise. She continued to mutter to herself. "These abandoned homes are dens for criminals, workplaces for prostitutes, and even hold roaming animals. There's also the threat of any Touched who may be in the area. Where is Garrett?"

Click, click, Anise heard her own footsteps on the street. She tried to keep focus but her mind wandered. She thought about why Garrett had been so impatient lately; he would have found that man on any other mission. He never lost control or attacked a training dummy in anger before. The thoughts nagged her. Why? This wasn't the Garrett she knew. What was going on?

"Hello there," a voice said. Anise turned to see three men emerging from a building behind her.

Her eyes darted from face to face looking at the men. She raised her dagger. They looked like normal humans. Anise was reluctant to release her aura. She backed away from them, keeping her focus on all three. "I don't want any trouble."

"We don't want trouble either," one man replied. "We're just looking for a little fun."

Anise smirked. "I'm not a fun girl."

"Only has to be fun for me, Sweets," the man replied.

Anise couldn't keep the shock from her face. "Did you just call me Sweets?"

The man nodded with a perverse smile. He licked his lips and advanced slowly. His friends walked forward but slightly sideways. They moved to encircle Anise.

As the men drew closer Anise stepped back and kept her dagger raised. These men were human. She stared at her dagger, the blade shining in the lamplight.

Only metal, no purple glow. She looked at the men, then back at her blade. She started to hum, then gently bit her lower lip. Her powers were for the Touched, not to use on the humans she tried to protect.

One man moved directly toward her, arms raised. Anise slashed her dagger from side to side, keeping the man at bay. Her head and eyes flashed side to side. The other two men surrounded her. She tried to back up but the two men moved too quickly. They each grabbed an arm. The one with her right arm squeezed her wrist until she dropped the dagger. It clattered as it hit the ground.

"Remember me?" the man in front of her asked.

Anise studied his face. She didn't recognize the face. She felt her body warming until she felt sweat dripping. "No. Who are you?" she managed to say keeping her composure.

The man glared right into her eyes. "An old target."

Anise tried to act oblivious. "Target?"

"We know you," he replied. "The streetwalker who drugs men and robs them. Your time has come. We want our money back."

Anise tried to pull away. "I have no money to give you."

The man licked his lips and grinned. "You'll pay us in trade."

The man bent down and picked up Anise's dagger. He toyed with it, waving the blade in front of her face. She began to tremble. Eyes widening, lip quivering, a look of terror came to her face.

"I d-don't know what y-you are talking a-about," she stammered, forcing a tear. Her eyes scanned the alley, looking for a way out.

The man thrust his free hand forward and grabbed Anise by the throat. "Don't act innocent!" His face reddened. His eyes bulged as he yelled the accusation. The force of the yell intensified Anise's trembling.

The man lowered the knife, slowly creeping it closer to Anise. "Hold her." The other men gripped Anise's arm tighter. Anise struggled against their hold but they held tight.

"I don't want to hurt you," Anise whimpered.

The man holding the knife raised it and waved the blade in front of her nose. "What could you do to hurt us?"

The man cut the left shoulder strap of Anise's dress. "Stop!" she screamed.

"Where's the fun in that?" the man asked. "I want what I paid for, now I intend to get it." He lowered the fabric off Anise's shoulder. He reached forward and undid the front of Anise's dress.

"Please," she pleaded. "Stop before something bad happens. I don't want to harm you."

The man holding her left arm chuckled. "You're in no position to harm anyone." He leaned over and licked Anise's neck.

The man holding her right arm took one hand and squeezed her breast through her dress. "I'm looking forward to this."

"Stop!" As Anise screamed her hair blackened, her skin colour changed, and her demonic aura began to glow. Purple light radiated in a sphere engulfing her body and the surrounding area.

Their eyes opened wide and their jaws dropped as the two men holding her let go and stepped back. The man in front dropped her dagger and stared. "What is this?"

Anise decided to use her aura to her advantage. While Anise spoke, her aura pulsed and her eyes glowed. "Hear me," she boomed. "Your actions will only lead to your demise. Leave me, leave this place, and never touch another hair on any woman's head."

The men ran off. As they ran Anise heard a voice. "Anise, what happened?" She turned to see Garrett gliding to a landing using his aura wings. "I could sense your aura. Are you hurt?"

Anise stared at him. "Some men looking for a streetwalker. Mistaken identity. I hope they learned their lesson."

Garrett dismissed his wings, but his hair and skin retained their orange hue. "I can't believe myself."

"What?" Anise asked as she closed her dress. She tied the strap in a knot on top of her shoulder.

"My temper," he muttered back. "We almost didn't find our initiate. I stormed off. Now you almost got hurt because of it."

"You're not feeling well," Anise offered. "No harm has come to anyone."

Garrett shook his head. "I feel like it's only a matter of time."

Anise smiled. "Let's go on another patrol. The fresh air will be a benefit, and the exertion of combat can give you a release."

Garrett nodded. They walked down the street away from the warehouse.

The clacking of their shoes on the hard stone echoed through the air. Garrett turned to Anise. "This old part of town is just decrepit."

"Not much here but rats, thieves, opium addicts, and streetwalkers," Anise replied. "That and the families who can't afford to live anywhere but a shack that's falling apart."

Garrett sniffed the air. "The new sanitation pipes get the smell of garbage and excrement out of the air in the new area."

"There's the smell of smoke from the factories in the new areas," Anise commented.

Garrett nodded. "There's also better public services in the new areas."

Anise stopped for a moment. She looked around. "This is an ideal hunting ground for the Touched though. Most people here could disappear unnoticed, deaths could be blamed on plagues and sicknesses."

The dim lights flickered and gave off an eerie glow. Unless directly under a streetlight, anyone would be a figure without a face. A slight chill in the night air made Anise shiver as the breeze tickled the back of her neck.

Two blocks down, a scraping noise broke the silence of night. Garrett raised his arm. "Did you hear that?"

"A scrape," Anise confirmed. "Someone's foot."

They approached the alleyway slowly. There were three figures near a wall. Larger than most humans, and slow-moving. The figures shuffled toward Anise and Garrett.

Garrett drew and readied his spear. "Shamblers."

Anise hummed. She shuddered and shook during her transformation. She drew her dagger and manifested her aura whip. Garrett took the lead followed by Anise. The buildings blocked the minuscule glow from the lamps along the street. Clouds covered the moon and stars. A complete absence of light left the alley pitch black.

The Shamblers moved toward them, arms up, in a wedge formation. Garrett charged the first Shambler, his spear flaming from his aura. He buried his spear in the chest of the front Shambler with ease.

Anise flicked her arm. Her DHEC aura whip wrapped around the Shambler on the left. It grabbed the crackling purple tether, struggling against Anise's hold. The Shambler on the right shuffled toward Garrett. The impaled Shambler grabbed the spear. Garrett wrestled for control. Twisting and jerking the shaft from side to side, the Shambler held firm. Beads of sweat formed on Garrett's brow. Each failed twist or torque was followed by a grunt. The Shambler held the spear and leaned back. Garrett dug his feet into the street. That did not stop his slow skid forward. The Shambler lifted a foot to step back. Garrett held firm. The two fought, maintaining a standstill.

"This one isn't dying," Garrett called out. "There's something different about it." He held the spear tight. The Shambler continued wrestling against him. Grunting, Garrett almost lost his grip on his weapon.

Anise's eyes darted back and forth. Her focus shifted. She lost control of her aura whip. The Shambler twisted, tugged, and jerked until Anise fell to the ground. Anise landed on her side. Her aura whip faded. The two Shamblers converged on Garrett.

Beads of sweat rolled down Garrett's face. He backed up, fighting for control of his spear. Anise came to one knee and channelled her whip again. She lashed it out and wrapped the legs of one Shambler; it tripped and fell forward.

Anise dismissed the whip. She rose to her feet, flicked her wrist, and lashed her whip across the face of the other Shambler. Its hand rose to cover the wound. "How do we kill them, Garrett?"

"I don't know," he grunted. "Maybe we need to channel more energy."

"Alright," Anise said. Bobbing her head, she began to hum and her arms vibrated. With her face and legs trembling, Anise's skin changed to its purple hue. Horns and wings sprouted. She pulled her dagger from its sheath and allowed the glowing purple energy to travel down the wavy blade.

Anise sprang into the air, gliding with her wings she tackled the Shambler holding Garrett's spear and plunged her dagger into its throat. The Shambler released the spear and stopped moving. He crumpled to the ground.

Garrett pulled his spear free. The other two Shamblers rose to one knee and lunged forward, landing on Anise.

"Anise!" Garrett screamed, his skin and aura burning orange. His black feathery wings emerged. His spear retracted to just a handle, then his DHEC energy burst forward, forming a large sword.

Garrett's glowing eyes shone through empty holes. His wings spread fully open. Sword in both hands, he sliced through both Shamblers in a single stroke. As Garrett brought the blade back up to a ready position both bodies separated into two pieces and slid off of Anise. No gore or blood exuded; the bodies were charred black along the laceration.

Anise knelt beside the bodies, running her hand along the darkened marks left by Garrett's sword. She glanced at Garrett with the massive orange blade in his hand. "They're seared."

Garrett's weapon dissolved as he stared at the sight before him. His eyes were wide and his mouth hanging open. Trembling, he stuttered, "H-how did I do that?"

Anise met Garrett's eyes. She pointed at his patron stone. "Your stone changed." It now had a head, arms, and legs; it was no longer an egg with open wings, it had taken the shape of a fury.

Turning on the ball of his foot, Garrett headed for the road. "I need to get back to the clutch."

"What's going on?" Anise asked.

"I feel sick," Garrett replied. "This new power...and there's a surging pain in my chest and stomach. I need...I need to get guidance. I must speak with Thraz immediately."

Following him, Anise looked back at the three bodies. Pulling out her glyph torch, she watched Garrett. She shook her head and hurried to reach him while tucking her torch back into her dress. She and Garrett continued down the road back to the warehouse.

"Where were you two?" Thraz barked, storming across the room to intercept them.

Garrett shook violently and looked desperately at Thraz. "Help me," he grunted, his arms and legs still shuddering.

"What in Hades' name happened out there?"

"We don't know," Anise explained. "There were three Shamblers. They attacked us. They...they weren't dying. They were on me. Garrett did some abnormal transformation. His power was awesome, but now he's unable to control himself."

"What kind of transformation?" Thraz asked.

"His aura created a sword from his spear handle, his wings emerged, skin colour changed, he seemed to lose control,"

Thraz nodded as she spoke. "Quickening."

"W-What?" Garrett stuttered while shivering.

"Quickening," Thraz repeated. "I haven't seen it in centuries. Happens when an Infernal creates a stronger DHEC connection with their patron stone and patron demon. Help me lay him down on that bench."

"Centuries?" Anise questioned as they shuffled to the bench.

"Demons have long lives," Thraz replied. "Now we need to concern ourselves with Garrett. Not every Infernal handles quickening well." Thraz knelt beside the bench.

Anise put her hand on her chest. "Was that what happened to me?"

"Not quite," Thraz grumbled. He glanced at Anise, met her eyes, and paused. "You awakened, fully. Your patron being Lilith, she drew you to the DHEC so strongly you were almost a true demon from the instant you Touched the stone. Garrett, and the others here, only managed to harness a glimpse of that power. Now Garrett is receiving more. Hopefully, he can handle it."

Thraz waved his arms slowly above Garrett's torso. The green glow of Thraz's aura began to emerge. Garrett's eyes closed. He stopped responding to the sounds in the room.

Anise stood silently looking on. Garrett's body convulsed. Thraz huffed and sweated as he worked on Garrett's condition. Sweat poured from Garrett; it soaked through his shirt. His face turned red. Anise simply stood there. She looked from Garrett to Thraz and back. She put her hand up to her face, made a fist, and gently bit her index finger.

"Is this my fault?" she whispered through her fist.

"No fault," Thraz said without taking his attention away from Garrett. "Quickening happens when it's triggered in a strong Infernal. Neither of you could have known. Couldn't have forced it either."

Thraz's aura continued to pulse. His sweat washed away his human façade. His skin colour and features morphed into his demonic form.

"Are you alright?" Anise asked.

"Just...can't hold my...transformation," Thraz grunted. His arms trembled. His aura engulfed his entire body. The green glow wafted and focused into an orb of demonic energy in his hands as they passed over Garrett's body. With one thrust of his arms, the green orb was shoved down. It expanded, encasing Garrett. The shaking and convulsing stopped. Thraz paused, his arms frozen in the orb of green light.

Thraz remained motionless for several moments. He didn't even appear to breathe. Anise watched intently. She went from biting her clenched fist to running her hands through her hair, and pacing.

"Is this really a quickening?" a voice asked.

Anise saw several Infernals drawn by the spectacle. "That's what Thraz said."

"Maybe that's why he was so hostile earlier," another voice added.

"I hope he pulls through," a third voice said. "I want to see what a full-powered Infernal looks like."

"Full-powered?" Anise questioned. Her eye twitched as she repeated the words. "He could be in grave danger and your concern is for a sparring partner?"

The instant Anise finished the words she shrieked. Her aura whip manifested and crackled in her hand. Her skin turned purple, her hair darkened to black, and horns sprang from her forehead. The purple succubus aura surrounded her. "Who wants to see a full-powered Infernal?"

The room fell silent. The crowd focused on Anise. "Who wants to see full power?" she repeated cracking her whip and stretching her wings.

The crowd backed away, many with wide eyes and open mouths. A few Infernals shuffled away and resumed their training. Most trained at quarter speed and watched Garrett. Anise made piercing eye contact with those gawking at Garrett. Her furious glare returned them to full-speed training.

Garrett's laboured voice managed to force out, "Ah-Anise."

Hearing the sound of his voice, Anise suppressed her demonic aura, her whip crackled and flashed as it disappeared. She turned away from the crowd and saw Thraz back to his human façade, slowly standing up. The green aura no longer encased Garrett as he lay on the bench.

"Garrett?" Anise started. "How are you?"

Garrett coughed. "I feel..." he coughed, "like someone threw, me against a brick wall a few dozen times."

Anise knelt beside him. The whites of his eyes were orange, his skin still had an orange hue. "Any answers?"

"It came to me," Garrett replied. "I'm like you; the spawn of a greater demon." He paused. His eyes stared blankly. His mouth started to open, then closed with an obvious clenching of his lips.

During Garrett's pause Anise waited, expecting him to continue. Finally, her impatience took over. "Which one?"

"Azazel. One of the first fallen angels."

Thraz set his hand on Anise's shoulder. "His power should be close to yours now, Anise."

Anise turned to Thraz. "Why didn't he have this before?"

"I don't know," Thraz replied. "When the quickening happens, it happens for a reason. Perhaps it was to protect you. It's possible it was his frustration with a strong foe. Maybe it was the anger from the exchange before he left earlier. There's also a chance it was a combination."

"Sounds so wise, so mysterious, but so inconclusive," Anise commented.

"Doesn't really matter," Thraz barked back. "It happened. It's done. We can't change it." Thraz walked away grumbling something undistinguishable under his breath.

"He has his moments," Garrett said.

"Moments?" Anise questioned.

Garrett sat up, struggling to keep steady. He held the bench with both hands for stability. "Some moments that demon can actually be pretty kind. It's unfortunate he has no patience."

Garrett tried to stand, but his legs wobbled. Anise caught him and sat him back on the bench. "You've been through a lot. Rest for now. We can explore your new power when you're ready."

Garrett nodded. "That's a good idea. Help me to bed."

Garrett put his arm around Anise's shoulders. He leaned on her as they shuffled to a room. Garrett crawled into the bed and fell asleep immediately. Spotting a barrel beside the wall, Anise sat down to watch over him.

Chapter 6 – Loyalty

"An imp?" Garrett questioned. "You want us to work with an imp?"

Thraz stared at him. "You need a team. He needs a mentor."

"He'll hold us back," Anise protested.

Roven stood there. His smile turned to a frown, his eyes started to water, and his lower lip began to tremble. "You seemed so nice when you brought me in," he whimpered.

"You were in a trance when we brought you in," Garrett snapped. "Thraz, you know I respect you, and your decisions, but he'll slow us down."

Thraz sighed. "Anise isn't made for pure combat like you are either, Garrett. She has many strong abilities, but they're not like yours. Roven's the same."

Garrett stepped back a few paces. He pulled the metal rod from his belt. It extended to form his spear. He swung, instantly reducing an empty barrel to kindling. "Are you saying all I'm good for is using this spear or my aura sword?"

Thraz held up his hand and waved it slightly. "Calm down. I didn't mean it that way..."

"What did you mean?" Garrett interrupted.

Thraz fell silent for a moment. His eyes darted back and forth. His head bobbed slightly. "Anise has her charms and her whip. She's not a soldier, but she can be excellent backup. Roven here can fill a similar role."

"Does that mean I don't get to fight?" Roven asked

Anise glared at him. "You think I don't fight?"

Roven backed up a few steps and raised his arms chest high with his palms open. "I didn't mean that." His voice trembled as he spoke.

"Stop! All of you." Thraz barked. "I need you all for this mission. My decision is final."

Garrett sighed. "What's the mission?"

"We need some intelligence gathered," Thraz replied. "Roven's abilities are ideal for this task. He'll need to train. His demonic abilities allow him access to restricted areas more discretely than your abilities do."

Garrett and Anise exchanged a quick glance then both turned to Roven. "You get in, and we back you up? Is that it?" Anise questioned.

Roven stood silently, looking to Thraz for direction.

"Not quite," Thraz said. "This is a two-part mission. You and Garrett are the known threat, Roven is the secret,"

Anise scrunched her face. "Known threat? Secret?"

Seeing he had their attention Thraz motioned for them all to sit down on some nearby cargo boxes. Once they were seated, Thraz began to explain.

"We have a report there's a group of full-blooded incubi and succubi working on a new form of Touched. We don't have many details. The group calls themselves the Bachysis; they couldn't decide whether to honour the name of the Roman Bacchus or Greek Dionysus. Anise, you can petition for membership as a succubus. Most of them have protectors; that's your role, Garrett. While they focus on you two Roven is to infiltrate and investigate."

Anise and Garrett grudgingly nodded.

Roven grinned with pleasure. "When do we leave?"

Thraz, looking at Garrett, then Anise, and finally Roven spoke. "You leave at sundown; get some rest."

"Thought you said training," Garrett said smugly.

Smugly Thraz got the last word as he walked away. "Help Roven work on his camouflage techniques for a while, but make sure you're rested. Succubus parties tend to run late and become wild."

Roven's eyes darted from Garrett to Anise and back. "I guess I should work on size and shape manipulation."

Garrett growled, "just do it. Make yourself small and unnoticeable enough to do your job. If we're apart, I can't save you."

Roven hummed and shuddered. He went from looking like a pot-bellied older man to a small cat; the hair stayed light grey with touches of white. "Meow," Roven said in his normal voice.

Garrett made a kicking motion but didn't actually hit Roven. "If you can't sound like the animal, don't give your disguise away by making noise..."

"Something smaller, quieter" Anise interrupted. "Can you make yourself a mouse?"

Roven's cat limbs twitched, he glowed a dull brownish yellow as he channelled the DHEC energy. The limbs changed and the body shrank. Roven finished in the form of a grey mouse.

"How long can you hold that shape?" Garrett asked. "Your DHEC stamina is still pretty low."

The mouse scurried around the floor. After about two minutes the limbs swelled. The limbs and body of the mouse grew and transformed back into Roven. "I guess...that's...my limit," he panted.

Garrett scoffed. "Two minutes. You better find some good hiding places. Try again. Let's see what your recovery time is."

Roven tried again. He returned to his mouse shape and held it slightly longer as he scurried around the room. Upon morphing back to his human form he was sweating profusely. "This is exhausting," he panted. "I need that rest Thraz mentioned."

"You also need to control DHEC energy better," Anise pointed out. "I'm usually not the hard one, but this is serious."

"DHEC DHEC DHEC," Roven began. "I made it through years of my life without this Demonic Heritage Energy Channel."

"What did you do anyway?" Garrett asked.

"I was a trader," he replied.

"What did you trade?" Anise asked.

Roven turned and faced Anise. "Whatever I could find; it was a very freelance existence."

Anise lifted her hand to interrupt. "We need that rest. Try to channel energy without transforming for a bit, then take a nap." She walked to a chamber and closed the door behind her.

Watching her walk away, Garrett and Roven went to find places to sleep.

*****

After resting they met with Thraz to be briefed. He took them off to one side of the room, a quiet corner. "The succubus lair is in an old storehouse by the last docks on the outskirts of the Old Quarter. We don't know who the leader is. All we know is they're working on a new form of Touched; it needs to be stopped."

Roven scratched his head. "Why are demons in the human realm making Touched?"

"They need a testing and hunting ground for the Touched to be proven in," Thraz replied. "Celestials are in this realm as well as Infernals. Touched are bred to fight for Hell's cause. Humans are here for them to turn. It's ideal and problematic at the same time."

"Do the Celestials know?" Garrett asked. "About the breeding attempt?"

Thraz shook his head. "No, and we intend to keep it that way. Full-blooded demons on Earth, breeding and developing Touched would be disastrous. Their presence gives full-blooded angels a reason to come down here. Angels and demons here on Earth would spark a war. We must prevent that."

"This is for the balance of power here in the human realm then?" Anise asked.

"Exactly," Thraz replied. "As strong as whatever this new Touched is or could be, and how beneficial it could prove in otherworldly wars, it does not belong here...at least not yet. We can't corrupt souls to fuel the armies of Hell if they're tainted by the Touched. We can't have our recruiting grounds impacted."

Garrett straightened up, adjusting and positioning his spear sheath. "We should go."

Anise nodded. Roven made eye contact with Thraz. Thraz waved his arm dismissing them. "Good luck."

Leaving the warehouse, Garrett took the lead. He walked so quickly Anise and Roven struggled to keep up. Even though Anise's dress had fewer layers than usual, it was still an encumbrance as she scurried to keep pace. Roven was sweating and trying to keep between a quick step and a jog to match Garrett's stride. They almost ran through the dock area. As they approached the last couple piers Garrett stopped. Anise slowed down and walked up to him. Roven jogged up and almost collapsed. He stood bent over with his hands on his knees breathing deeply.

"We split up here," Garrett instructed. He stared at Roven then pointed. "You work your way up to that building with the light in the windows and try not to make so much noise breathing. Anise and I will be entering through the front door."

Roven nodded. "I may be able to find a way in through one of the dark windows." He skulked away using crates and buildings as cover.

"Do you need to be so hard on him?" Anise asked. "He's new, he isn't well trained yet, but at least he's trying. He just wants some approval."

Garrett sighed. "If we aren't hard on him he won't learn. You had to work to control your powers. I've done extensive weapons training. He's lived a trader's life. They're all talk, he needs more. He can do more. Let's get this done."

Garrett ended the discussion by walking away. Anise caught up and walked beside him. She tilted her head towards his with a gleam in her eye. "I'm the succubus, I should be in front. You're the bodyguard."

"I'm not sure I like the smugness of that tone," Garrett replied. "You are correct though." Garrett slowed his pace for a few steps and followed two paces behind Anise as they approached the door.

Reaching the door, Anise discovered it was barred from the inside. A small piece of wood slid open around eye level. Someone looked out. His voice was rough and aggressive. "Who goes there?"

"My name is Anise. I've come to petition for membership."

The eyes shifted slightly and locked on Garrett. "What about him?"

Anise said, "my bodyguard. I wouldn't want to be out all alone with those Celestials wandering around."

The eyes went up and down, most likely a nod. "You speak true, sister. Come in, we'll show you around."

The door opened. The instant she was in the man behind the door started patting down her dress. Anise widened her eyes and opened her mouth trying to feign shock at being searched.

"I'm surprised you're searching for me."

"Can never be too careful," he said brushing through the folds and ruffles, patting and pressing until he felt the body beneath. His eyes looked up and he drew Anise's kris dagger. "Especially when people want to bring in hidden weapons."

"Even when accompanied by a bodyguard a girl needs something to defend herself," Anise said innocently. Garrett walked forward and silently handed his spear to the doorman.

The doorman looked at Garrett with a raised eyebrow. "This small rod everything?"

Garrett snatched the spear and extended it to full length. He ran his aura through it. The spear glimmered orange for a moment. The doorman's eyes widened; he gulped. Garrett dismissed the energy flowing through the spear, retracted it to its small size, and handed it back to the doorman. "If your security is unprepared for my weapons, my lady is fortunate to have me."

The doorman's mouth twitched. He made a low growling noise. "You may enter. Visitors go to the second door on the right and wait for a member to greet them properly." He stepped back and motioned for Anise and Garrett to proceed.

Slowly, Anise walked down the dim, candle lit hallway. Garrett followed behind her; his eyes never stopped checking the hallway. In the room, they found a couple of wooden benches and some padded chairs.

"Benches," Garrett muttered. "I thought succubi and incubi were pleasure-oriented demons."

Anise pointed to each piece of furniture and her mouth moved as she counted. "There are four benches and four padded pieces. Probably intended for the new initiate and their protector."

Garrett walked to the wall. He stood with his back to it, watching the doorway out of sight. "A real protector wouldn't sit with his back to the entrance."

Anise walked over to a chair that faced the door. "I suppose I'm intended to sit." She sat down facing the door.

"Four sets of seats," Garrett mused. "Do they expect four petitioners with bodyguards at once? Or will there be three interviewers?"

Anise scratched her head. "We'll know when someone comes in."

They were left alone for several minutes. Anise managed to stay sitting. Garrett paced, keeping his focus on the door.

"A new initiate?" a voice questioned. A moment later a man walked into the room. He was slender, with dark hair, average height, and wearing black pants, a white shirt with a ruffled cravat in the middle, and a loose-fitting, knee-length purple coat.

Anise went to stand. The man raised his hand and walked to a chair across from hers. "Stay sitting child. There's no ceremony requiring you to stand for me."

"I thought I was being polite," Anise replied sheepishly.

The man chuckled. "Polite in our world is different from polite out there." He pointed to a window and paused. His head and body spun when he noticed Garrett in the corner near the window. "A protector? Or another one of us?"

"Who are you?" Garrett demanded.

"Quiet!" Anise snapped. "I'll ask the questions."

"Yes, my lady," Garrett said reluctantly but obediently.

Anise turned her attention back to the man. "He does pose a valid question. What is your name?"

The man put his hand up to his cravat and played with the ruffles for a moment. "Call me Crevan."

Anise nodded. "I've come to seek an organization of others like me. Would that be you?"

"Like you how?" Crevan asked coyly. "Young like you? A lady like you? Less of a "lady"." He paused and winked.

Garrett straightened up, clenching his fist. Anise merely chuckled. "I suppose less of a lady could be accurate." At Anise's laugh, Garrett relaxed his hand and stood easier.

"Your protector," Crevan said with a nod. "He provokes easily. He will be most...amusing."

"Amusing?" Garrett questioned.

"Down in our halls," Crevan replied. "We have our members and our protectors. Our protectors also serve as some of our entertainment."

Anise leaned forward. "Entertainment?"

"We should redirect this conversation," Crevan said. "Before you enter our halls, we must assess your worthiness. Who is your family?"

Anise closed her eyes and reopened them. "I'm an orphan."

"I don't mean your family among the mortals," Crevan laughed. "I mean your demonic family. Who is your patron?"

"Lilith."

Crevan's eyebrows rose. "The queen herself?"

"Yes. She communed with me when I first channelled the DHEC. She is my..."

"Anise," Garrett interrupted.

"Your what?" Crevan asked.

"Patron," Anise replied. "Garrett, what did you want?"

"Sorry," Garrett muttered. "I thought I heard something."

"What can you channel?" Crevan asked.

Anise stood. She hummed and her limbs vibrated. She allowed her aura to encase her body. Her skin colour took on a slight purple tinge and her hair turned black. She allowed her wings to spread. She took on her demonic form but did not manifest her aura whip. "This is my transformation."

"Impressive," Crevan commended. "What about him?"

Garrett closed his eyes. He released his orange aura around him. He didn't spread his wings or channel his aura into a weapon form.

"Furies make good protectors," Crevan commented. He walked over and circled Garrett while assessing him. "Impressive wingspan. The wings, in general, are very nice; excellent colour, and pristine feathers. Good strong flow from the aura. Very nice indeed."

A woman entered the room. "Excuse me, Crevan. I need to speak with you a moment."

Crevan stepped back toward the door. Raising a finger he said, "I'll return as soon as I can."

Crevan stepped outside. With the door ajar, Anise saw Crevan standing there. Mumbled sounds hummed in from the hall, but nothing loud or clear enough to make out the words. Anise and Garrett dismissed their auras. Anise sat back in the chair. Garrett walked to one of the wooden benches and sat down.

Words weren't needed. They exchanged a few glances while Crevan was out. They were both concerned about Roven. Had he been caught already?

Crevan came back in and went to his chair. He sat and adjusted his position. He was slouching in the padded chair, quite relaxed. "Excuse the interruption."

"You're a busy man," Anise replied. "No apology is necessary."

"Where were we?" Crevan asked as he scratched his cheek. "Ah yes, a succubus and a fury. You both have nice wings and strong auras. I'm certain there is sufficient evidence for a membership attempt."

Anise smiled. "Excellent news. What is required to petition for membership?"

"First," Crevan said, "you should see our halls. Ensure you are ready for us before you attempt our trials."

Anise met Garrett's eyes and he nodded. They both stood. Anise extended her arm toward the door. "We're ready when you are."

Crevan sauntered to the door. "Follow me then."

Crevan led them down the hall and through the final door on the left. A spiral staircase descended below the warehouse. At the bottom of the steps, a small hallway led to a double door. Crevan stood at the door. He put one hand on each door, inhaled, and flung the doors open as he exhaled.

The instant Crevan went through the door he tore off his coat; he wasn't wearing a shirt at all. The coat provided an image of one where none existed. He stood there in his trousers and cravat, turned his head, and simply said, "welcome."

Anise walked into the large room. Padded furniture sat in groups all around the large room. Columns rose from the floor to the high ceilings. Lit by torches, glas screens shaded with red and purple cast a hew over the different areas. The fabrics were a mixture of reds, blues, and purples. Suddenly Anise sneezed. In awe of the gigantic room, she hadn't noticed the strong mixture of perfume smells assaulting her nose.

"Smells stronger than the bath chamber of a brothel in here," Anise commented.

Garrett nodded. "Looks like one too." He waved his arm around stopping to point out the outfits in the room. Many of the men were without shirts, several wore short pants instead of full-length. Many of the ladies were wearing short skirts, blouses were open or crumpled beside them, and their undergarments were either red or purple lace or black leather. Hands roamed across the mass of people, touching, stroking, caressing. Individuals fed finger foods to one another.

Crevan spun around. "Welcome to the room of delights. Here we focus on our pleasures. Mingle as you wish and enjoy your stay."

Garrett stood stunned for a while. "I'm amazed something so lush and hedonistic exists under such a rat hole of a building."

Crevan chuckled. "The best pleasure palaces are the best hidden. Go on, find your fill; we have food, wine, ale, women, men, whatever your pleasure."

"Men?" Garrett repeated with shock.

"Remember Garrett," Anise started. "This is a pleasure room, and these demons have been doing this since that armour of yours was fashionable. They've seen and done things you can't even imagine."

Anise swaggered forward demonstrating high confidence. She took a piece of fruit from a bowl and then rubbed it on the lips of a nearby incubus. He wrapped his arms around her and dragged her to the bed. Garrett took a few commanding steps forward to intervene, but Crevan reached out, putting a hand to his chest.

"She chose to initiate that," Crevan said. "You would be wise to learn when to act as a protector and when to enjoy yourself."

Garrett scowled. He kept his eyes fixed on Anise. "A true guardian is one who remains vigilant and alert even in seemingly safe circumstances."

Crevan chuckled. "I assure you such measures are unnecessary."

Garrett stared straight into Crevan's eyes. "I only just met you. I do not know you. I do not know your people. Pardon me for saying this, but performing my duty requires me to distrust you."

Crevan shuddered at the words. He composed himself. "You speak well. I take no offence, and be assured I meant to offer none."

Garrett returned to watching Anise. She moved to a large mattress and shared grapes with a small group. Feeding grapes to each another one at a time, they laughed while caressing arms and legs throughout the mass of bodies. The odd grape fell to the floor ignored by those caught up in their revelry. Garrett's lip twitched as he watched intently. He scrutinized Every move of a hand toward Anise.

"You're awful diligent," a voice said from behind Garrett.

He didn't flinch. "As her protector, that is my task."

"You should enjoy yourself," the voice protested.

Garrett sighed. "Who are you?" With a huff, he turned to see a succubus wearing a barely buttoned half blouse exposing her stomach, and tight black pants which didn't reach as far as her knees.

"Serena," she replied. "I'm known here by many of the protectors. I ensure they are fully able to embrace their passionate desires."

Garrett returned his focus to Anise. "I have no desire for you."

"Your friend will be here a while," Serena said. "Do you intend to stand in stoic solitude until she is done? Wouldn't you rather explore your own desires?"

Garrett growled. His hands clenched into fists, which he quickly released. "My sole intention is to protect and guard her. If that means standing watch all night then that's what it means. If it means dying defending her against an onslaught of your kind, I'll take as many of you down with me as I can." As he finished speaking, he tilted his head and cocked a half smile aimed at Serena.

Her eyes flashed. "How dare you?"

"How dare I what?" Garrett questioned without lifting his gaze.

"No protector has ever refused me," Serena stated. "I won't have a blemish on my record from the likes of a mere Infernal like you." She reached over and stroked his cheek with the back of her finger.

Garrett flinched. "Leave me to my duties. Find another consort for the evening."

"Evening?" Serena scoffed. "You protectors don't last more than an hour before I lose interest."

"Then why do you even chase me?" Garrett asked. "If we protectors are so poor at holding your interest, then one would think you'd have moved on to something else."

Serena scowled. "I have my way with them so I may say they were mine."

"Trophies?" Garrett questioned. "I'm afraid I won't be a fixture in your display."

With a huff, Serena turned and stormed off.

"You speak well," Crevan observed. "You could have had her, and some enjoyment, this night."

Garrett shook his head. "I'm here for Anise. It's difficult enough not to act when I see her interacting in such a manner with those people out there."

"Demons," Crevan corrected. "Those are not average people, they're demons. Many who find their sinful pleasures here can trace their adventures back as far as the Bacchanalia, some even earlier."

"Bacchanalia?" Garrett repeated.

"Roman festivals celebrating the god Bacchus," Crevan replied. "Those were fun times. Wine, music, dancing, and of course, a little mischief."

Gritting his teeth, Garrett made a growling noise under his breath. His arm slowly moved toward the sheath on his back, but he remembered it was empty and returned his arm to his side. After a moment he crossed his arms.

While Garrett and Crevan spoke, Anise moved through four groups of succubi. She sauntered back to Garrett. Her dress was open, the inner skirt was gone; she looked half-dressed.

"This has been very entertaining," Anise said with a slight giggle. "I've had some interesting offers made to me. Crevan, would you excuse us?"

Crevan bowed and stepped backward. "Of course, excuse me." He straightened up and walked away.

"I wonder how Roven is doing," Anise whispered. "They're too decadent for me. I can't behave this way much longer."

"Agreed," Garrett grumbled in a low voice. "It's hard to even stand here and observe. I've had to use a lot of control to avoid lunging at those who play with you too...familiarly."

"You really do care," Anise joked.

Garrett's eyes narrowed as he stared at Anise. "I've always cared," he snapped. "That was a large part of why I quickened."

Anise smirked and shook her head. "We still need to get information on the new Touched. These succubi are hard to probe for anything of substance because they only concern themselves with their enjoyment."

"One tried to pursue me," Garrett said. "She seemed quite offended when I rejected her."

Anise's eyes widened. "Impressive restraint."

"We're here on a mission," Garrett replied. "We just need to keep them occupied here so Roven can search."

Anise smirked. "I guess it's back to..."

"A moment of your time please," Crevan interrupted.

"A moment," Anise replied with a coy smile. "I want to rejoin the fun."

"That will have to wait," Crevan replied. "I need you both to come with me."

Anise and Garrett exchanged glances. They nodded and followed Crevan. He led them out of the room and back to one of the meeting rooms in the main hallway. Crevan pushed the door open and motioned with his arm for Anise and Garrett to enter.

Roven was tied to a wooden armchair. His clothing was torn, his left eye was swollen shut, his lip and nose bled. He sat there almost motionless; the only sign he hadn't been killed was a low whimpering noise. As they took in the sight a tear ran down Roven's face.

"What is this?" Garrett asked sharply. "You show us a room of pleasure, and then some man beaten half to death."

"We couldn't kill him yet," a voice said from the shadows behind Roven's chair. Two large men emerged. They weren't men. Their skin had a reddish-orange glow, they had large black feathered wings.

"Furies," Anise gasped.

"We have our protectors too," Crevan said.

"Is this some initiation for me?" Garrett asked trying to sound confused. "You show us the pleasure side of this succubus organization, and now you show us how you can take such pleasure because your protectors are carrying out the less desirable tasks?" As he finished, he exhaled deeply. It took Garrett a moment to calm his breathing.

Crevan shook his head. "You misunderstand. We caught this spy, an Infernal no less, creeping around in our building. It seems odd that two Infernals appear and say they seek membership on the same evening one enters our lair and starts skulking around. Don't you agree?"

"Mer-cy," Roven coughed. The cough brought blood which oozed down his chin and dripped onto his chest.

"Is he with you?" Crevan asked.

"Why would I want to work with someone so pitiful?" Garrett asked, avoiding the actual question.

"He doesn't seem to be on our level, does he, *Garrett*?" Anise asked.

Garrett saw her eyes and realized she intended him to use her name for Roven to hear. "No, Anise. He seems nowhere near our level."

"Gar-rett?" Roven panted. "A-nise?"

"He seems to know you?" Crevan observed.

"He's just repeating names in his state," Anise said. "I've drugged humans before; when their minds aren't clear they say random words or repeat what was just said."

Crevan smiled. "He's Infernal, not human. He already gave up your names. I was offering you the chance to be honest with me. There are two options now. First, due to your auras and the power I perceived, I can offer you the chance to join us, you'll be under severe scrutiny for some time to ensure loyalty, but you'll be in good company. Second, you may refuse my offer and end up like your friend."

"You accuse us of being spies, then you offer us admission?" Garrett asked. "Aside from what I'm assuming is an offer of safe treatment, how would we benefit from joining?"

"As our clan grows our power grows," Crevan replied. "Why do demons do anything? For their benefit. I believe we can benefit from your abilities being added to our clan."

Garrett assessed the room. Two furies flanked Roven in the chair, and Crevan, presumably an incubus. Unarmed, Garrett and Anise had only their auras as weapons.

Anise broke the moment of silence. "You told us how your clan benefits. What benefit exists for us?"

"As we grow, you grow with us."

"And what are we using that strength for?" Anise continued. "What tangible gains are to be realized?"

Crevan chuckled. "My dear, you know the war persists. You know the gates of Heaven remain under constant siege. Our demonic lords will reward those who breach the walls handsomely. We will offer our lords an army."

"An army of two initiates and a room full of lust-driven succubi?" Anise questioned with a hint of sarcasm.

"We will have more," Crevan assured her. "Once the army's grown we will be a clan to be reckoned with."

"If it isn't succubi, and Infernals aren't going to be useful against full-blooded angels, then what's left?" Garrett asked.

"Shifters," Crevan replied. "The newest evolution of the Touched." Crevan sounded delighted and maddened as he spoke. "Shifters," he repeated. "Capable of assuming an incorporeal state to pass through walls and barriers, feeding on the life energy of their foes through touch, there one moment and gone the next?"

"How do you control something like that?" Garrett asked. "Wouldn't it turn on you to feed? Your weapons would pass right through it."

Crevan laughed like a lunatic. He raised his arms in front of him and his fingers curled into claws. "We bred them like Shamblers, weak against DHEC energy. We use the same channel you do. They can feed on the humans and swell their ranks while we wait in pleasure and comfort for an army to be amassed." His breath ran short as he finished. Once he inhaled, Crevan began laughing uncontrollably.

Anise looked at Garrett. "Time for us to go."

Garrett nodded. They both hummed and shuddered. Garrett's large aura sword manifested in his hand. The blaze of orange lit the room. Anise flicked out her arm and her aura whip crackled while purple sparks popped around it.

Anise lashed her whip through the air in the room. Crevan and the furies backed up. Once he saw an opening, Garrett darted forward and used his sword to cut Roven's bonds and flung the limp body over his shoulder.

"Let's go!" Garrett shouted. He sprang through the door into the hallway and sprinted to the door. It was sealed. He began hacking at it with his aura sword as Anise ran backward lashing her whip at their pursuers.

Pieces of the door splintered off, but metal bands reinforced the wood. Garrett growled and panted at the slow process of slashing at the door.

"The lock," Anise called. "Break the lock."

Garrett plunged the tip of his sword into the door closure. The metal pieces fell to the ground. Garrett threw the door open and ran out into the daylight. Anise jumped out after him. The furies pursuing them came to the threshold but stayed inside.

Anise stopped flicking her whip around. "They stopped at the door."

Garrett dropped Roven on the ground and took his sword handle in both hands. The aura blade grew. "Don't let your guard down. It could be a ploy."

Suddenly Thraz appeared between the furies. "Enough," he said.

"Thraz?" Anise asked. "What's going on?"

"You and Garrett are strong enough now we needed to test you. Would you be loyal to the clutch, or to the promise of power?"

"What about Roven?" Garrett asked pointing to the limp body on the ground.

Roven stood up. "Imp DHEC. I used my camouflage techniques."

Anise and Garrett stared at Thraz. They dismissed their weapons while they took a moment to catch their breath.

"A setup?" Anise questioned. "Why?"

"Loyalty," Thraz replied. "I need to know I can trust you no matter what."

"You're unbelievable," Garrett said. "How can you toy with people this way?"

"Be mad if you want," Thraz said. "I deserve your rage now. Your understanding can come later."

Chapter 7 - Friction

Garrett stormed away. His brisk pace only slightly less than a jog.

Anise glared at Thraz. "He's furious."

Thraz nodded. "I know. As I said, for now, I deserve his rage. You better go after him."

"Why me?" Anise questioned.

"You're the only one he's going to listen to," Thraz replied. "You're the level-headed one."

"I'll go too," Roven said. "Anise might need some help."

Anise shook her head. "I doubt you'll be useful, but come on. Weapons?"

Crevan turned to one of the furies behind him. The man disappeared and almost instantly returned carrying Anise's dagger and Garrett's spear handle. He handed them to Anise. She sheathed the dagger and scurried down the street, both hands raising the front of her dress and one scrunching the spear handle into the fabric. Roven jogged to catch her. Once he caught up he kept pace.

"Where will he go?" Roven asked.

"He's angry," Anise replied. "He doesn't know where he's going. He's just putting distance between him and Thraz."

After a couple blocks, Anise stopped. She put her hand over her chest, closed her eyes, and started to think about Garrett. Her patron stone glowed faintly from beneath her dress, but Roven spotted it.

"Trying to track him?" Roven asked

"Shhh," Anise hushed.

"Sorry, I just asked."

Anise opened her eyes. "I'm not very adept at this yet. I need to concentrate."

"You don't need to snap at me," Roven said.

"You barely fight, your camouflage and hiding are at a fledgling level, and you're hardly even a trickster. Despite all that you came to support me, support how?"

Roven stared at his hands, then at his feet. "It's true, I have to manifest my abilities, but I need to be tested to do that. When have I had the chance? When were my abilities useful? Where was I needed?"

Anise let out a moan and returned to her tracking attempt. Her chest glowed. She stood still for a moment then opened her eyes. She pointed. "He's over there. I sense his energy."

Anise rushed down the street, Roven on her heels. They turned a corner to see Garrett engulfed in his bright orange aura, with wings fully expanded.

"Garrett!" Anise shouted.

He backed up but didn't change his focus from whatever was in front of him. Anise could feel a chill in the air. She channelled energy and began to glow. Her aura expanded out. She summoned her wings and whip. Anise cautiously crept forward. She had Garrett's spear handle in her hand. As the two met she handed the weapon to him. Garrett immediately took the handle in both hands and channelled his aura sword. Garrett kept himself between Anise and whatever was there. Anise stepped to the side to see around Garrett's wings.

"What are those?" she exclaimed. The sight before her was completely unknown. Two figures, cloaked in tattered black robes. Hoods covered their heads and faces. A black smoke-like aura surrounded their bodies. It came away from them, flickering like an uncountable number of small black candle flames. There was no sign of legs or feet. No sound of contact with the ground. They appeared to be floating, hovering, in front of Garrett.

"They're some kind of Touched," Garrett said. "I caught them bearing down on a couple of vagrants. Looked like they planned to infect the poor men."

The figures made no noise as they listed toward Garrett. He channelled his aura through his spear. The bright orange glare lit up the alley more than the rising sun. With a lunge, Garrett buried his spear in the abdomen of the figure before him. Without any sign of reaction, the creature continued to float forward.

Anise jogged forward. She started lashing her whip toward both figures. The purple light from her whip twinkled as it passed through the robed figures. "What are they?" she shouted.

Roven stepped up. He pulled a small chain from his pocket. It glowed with a dull yellowish-brown light. The glow was barely visible. Channelling the DHEC into his weapon was sluggish, his breathing laboured. He gasped while darting in. He strung the chains around the robed figures. As he ran, his chain floated around them. As he went along the chain expanded. When Roven stopped, he gave a tug. The chains tightened and clattered to the ground in a heap.

"If our weapons don't work, what else do we have?" Anise shouted.

Garrett flapped his wings. Strong gusts blew toward the cloaked figures; the air current passed through them. "I guess we can't even push them back with our wings," he growled.

Roven collected his chain and started running around the figures again. Garrett backed up, noticed Roven and observed; his eyebrows raised as he watched. Anise tried wrapping her whip around one of the figure's hoods, but it went right through. With his attention diverted to Roven, Garrett didn't notice the figure had drifted to within arm's length. What appeared to be an arm, with waves of the same smoky aura, arced up, and a finger extended toward Garrett's face.

Garrett noticed the arm. He raised his spear but then froze. His face went blank. His eyes stared forward. His arms and legs didn't even twitch.

"Garrett!" Anise yelled.

Silence.

"Garrett," Roven called.

Again, silence.

The figure's finger crept toward Garrett's face. The flickering black cloak subsided. Garrett stood paralyzed until the figure touched him. At the moment of contact, Garrett's aura vanished. His wings disappeared. He stood there, motionless, silent, and devoid of facial expression.

"Try now," Roven said, giving his chain a yank. As the chains tightened around the figure, the body solidified. Anise flicked her arm and wrapped her whip around the hood of the figure, it held. The figure resisted her. It fought. It howled. The shrill cry was neither man nor beast. Anise put both hands on her whip and Roven tugged his chain while jumping backward. They pulled the figure away from Garrett.

In a cloud of smoke, the figure vanished. The second figure turned and retreated. At the rear of the alleyway, it passed through a solid stone wall.

Garrett dropped to his knees, the blank stare still present on his face. His spear fell to the ground and retracted to just the handle. Anise rushed over and knelt beside him. Her whip and aura faded.

"Garrett?" she asked. "Can you hear me?" She waved her hand in front of his eyes. Garrett's focus never changed; his eyes didn't follow her motions.

Roven approached while putting his chain away. "How is he?"

"He doesn't respond," Anise choked while trying to force back tears.

Anise put her hand on Garrett's face. "He's cold." She glanced at Roven who stood over her looking around the alley.

"Where did that other one go?" Roven asked, his eyes darting around. "We should get out of here before it comes back."

"We can't just leave him!" Anise ground out as the tears slowly trickled down her face. "He does so much for us. We can't leave him like this." She bent over Garrett's body and hugged him. "His whole body is cold." A tear ran down her cheek.

"I'd go for help, but I think it unwise to leave you alone if that creature returns," Roven said.

"He's too heavy to carry," Anise stated. "We need help, or we wait for him to wake up."

Garrett's body started to quiver. Anise jumped off. Garrett shivered and shook, limbs twitching. His entire body convulsed, violently at first then the severity lessened to a constant shiver. "Cold," he whispered.

"He's, he's alive," Anise sighed with relief.

"Creatures, where?" Garrett whispered.

"We defeated one, the other fled," Roven said.

"How?" Garrett asked, his voice returning to normal volume.

"When it touched you, its cloak vanished, our weapons worked," Roven replied.

"Can you stand?" Anise asked.

"I'll try," Garrett groaned, struggling to sit up. "I feel weak and cold. I'm having trouble channelling the DHEC for strength too."

Anise and Roven's eyes met with an exchange of worried expressions. They each took an arm and helped Garrett to his feet. They walked out of the alleyway and turned toward the warehouse.

"We need to get to the clutch," Anise said. "Thraz can help with your wounds, we need to report this creature. It's been a long time since any of us had any sleep."

Garrett's face said the words his mouth left unspoken. He didn't want to see Thraz right now, his face flushed with rage. He stifled his objection and allowed Anise and Roven to support his weight as they walked back to the clutch. Dawn broke. People started leaving their homes and walking to the factories. Whistles summoning the workforce blew in the distance. Even in the Old Quarter, there were some who gave them puzzled looks, but none stopped to question or offer aid; they had their own lives to live.

When they entered the warehouse, the Infernals were assembled around Thraz. Standing on a shipping crate, he addressed the entire clutch. "We need to use the soul-binding glyph more often," he said. "Our goal here is to save the souls of the humans from the Touched so their souls are untainted and can fuel the armies of Hell. Offer assistance in exchange for payment." Thraz waved his arms as he spoke. "The payment comes later. Offer them the protection of the glyph. Tell them it's a religious token, a way to protect against those creatures and monsters."

"The soul-binding glyph?" Roven whispered to Anise.

"It's meant for binding souls to Hell," Anise explained. "We save people, but we can also mark them. I'm sure you heard of a deal with the devil. This is that deal, but with one of his agents in his stead."

A puzzled expression crossed Roven's face. "Why have I never seen this glyph before? It sounds as though it should be one of the first glyphs we're taught."

Anise motioned toward a chair. She answered as they shuffled over and deposited Garrett. "It seems to have fluctuated in importance over time. I was shown early on, but we haven't been presented with the expectation to use it at every opportunity. Garrett barely bothers with glyphs at all."

Thraz continued to talk. He took out a glyph torch and demonstrated the soul-binding glyph. Roven locked his eyes on the torch in Thraz's hand. Thraz started with the infinity sign, then swirled the torch creating a five-loop spiral through it and finished with a circle around the design. "This is it," he said. "Infinity, bound five times, and closed in an unending circle." He put the glyph torch away.

After putting the torch away Thraz spotted Anise and Roven. "Dismissed," he barked. As the crowd dispersed Thraz walked over. His pace quickened once he saw Garrett slumped over in a chair.

He stopped a few steps short of the chair. "What happened?"

"Some shadowy figures were in an alleyway," Anise began. "Garrett was fighting them without weapons, his aura and wings were out. We managed to get him his spear but it was ineffective..."

"How?" Thraz interrupted.

"It passed through, but there was no effect," Anise replied.

"What did these figures look like?" Thraz asked.

"They floated," Roven began. "Black cloaked figures, with hoods, without any sign of feet. They..."

"They approached and he froze?" Thraz interrupted again.

"Exactly," Anise agreed. "One extended an arm and Garrett just stopped. Once he was touched, he dropped his spear and his aura faded away."

"How did you deal with it?" Thraz asked.

"When it touched Garrett the flickering black aura around it went away. My chains could hold it then," Roven replied.

"Was the air around it cold?" Thraz asked.

Anise tilted her head, trying to remember. "Garrett said something about feeling cold when he was able to whisper to us. I didn't notice anything. I was focused on Garrett."

Thraz reached out for Garrett, the green glow of his aura extending from his hands. The glow wafted around Garrett's face and then formed a murky green bubble around his head.

Thraz hummed for a moment. "You stopped it just in time."

"Stopped what!" Anise demanded.

"In a second," Thraz snapped. "Let me work, I'll explain after."

Thraz closed his eyes. His hands swayed as he channelled healing energy around Garrett's head.

"Focusing on just his head," Roven whispered to Anise.

"That thing's finger was pointing to his face," Anise replied. "Maybe whatever's wrong is all in Garrett's head."

Garrett's eyes blinked. His head shifted as he assessed his surroundings. His eyes flashed. He reached forward and grabbed Thraz by the wrist. "What did you set up this time?"

Thraz shook off the grip and stepped back. "I didn't set this up; I wouldn't."

"How can we be sure?" Garrett questioned. "Our last mission was a fake. A setup. How can I be sure whatever that thing was tonight isn't part of some larger plan? Some plan to enrage me in order to make me see I need you? Get me sick from that cold, uh, whatever it was, and you conveniently have the cure..."

"Garrett," Anise tried to sooth him. "You need to rest and recover." She put her hand on his shoulder.

Garrett shook her hand away. "Roven too. He was there. I saw everything. As soon as I was frozen his chains worked. What stopped them before? What act is he putting on this time?"

"It's no act," Roven tried to assure him. "I don't know what that was either."

"Lies!" Garrett screamed, forcing himself to his feet.

"Garrett," Anise pleaded, "settle yourself. You're not well after that ordeal. You need to rest."

Garrett stumbled. "How can I rest?" He put his hand to his forehead. "I don't know what to believe."

"Believe in me," Anise replied, putting her hands on his shoulders. Her face inches from his, she stared into his eyes with conviction. "You were here for me when I awakened. My being in danger caused your quickening. We're partners. I put my life in your hands all the time; know you can do the same."

Garrett sighed. He let out a grumble and sat back in the chair. "Alright, what was that creature?"

"Shifter," Thraz said as he sat on a barrel. Anise and Roven sat on a crate. "They're a dangerous type of Touched. They shift from corporeal to incorporeal; that's where they get their name from."

"Corporeal? Incorporeal?" Anise sounded confused.

"Corporeal means having a physical form," Thraz explained. "Shifters can shift into a state where they seem real to looking like an illusion. They have no substance at that time, that's incorporeal."

"Are they demonic in nature?" Roven asked.

"They were bred by demons," Thraz answered. "That's why your DHEC energy was effective when they became corporeal and you made contact."

"How do we make contact?" Roven asked. "My chain fell right through the Shifter, but the next time it held."

"What did you notice?" Thraz asked.

"It was black," Roven answered. "Floating, it had no feet. An aura flickered off it like small black candle flames. It went after Garrett. It moved slowly. It extended an arm toward him. That was when the chain worked when Garrett was already attacked."

"Did you see or feel anything else?" Thraz asked.

"It felt cold," Garrett said. "It chilled me right to the bone. I couldn't see eyes, but I could feel a gaze staring right through me..."

"The cloak disappeared," Anise blurted out. "When the weapons worked the aura was suppressed."

"You three are getting smarter," Thraz commented. "That's the key with Shifters. Their aura subsides when they are corporeal. That's when you can hit them."

"The one dropped its aura to attack Garrett," Roven said. "He was already paralyzed when the cloak dropped. Are you saying we need to sacrifice someone or use someone as bait? How can we do that? Is there a protective glyph? How many Infernals with reaper heritage are here to go out as a team healer? We may not always make it back here in time. These things are too dangerous..."

Thraz reached out and grabbed Roven. "Stop babbling!" Thraz adjusted in his seat while the other three stared at him. "We have ways. Never lose your calm."

Roven sulked, crossing his arms. Thraz's head shook slightly as his eyes met Garrett's

"Roven deserved it," Garrett said, "but he is correct. They are dangerous, extremely dangerous."

"I need you to develop," Thraz said.

"Develop?" Garrett questioned. "Anise and I awakened our powers in ways you said you hadn't seen for centuries. We've developed beyond anyone else here. How much more can our powers develop?"

"Such arrogance," Thraz groaned. "For you to believe you're developed to a point where growth is no longer a possibility, I don't understand you sometimes."

"It's like I said, Anise's and my patron stones have fully transformed into a demonic form instead of the eggs most carry. We can manipulate our auras in ways far beyond the others here. We're another level of Infernal."

Thraz sighed. "By comparison, your demonic powers are stronger than others around you, yes. But I'm not talking about your wingspan, your aura weapons, your demonic transformations, I'm talking about your minds."

"Are you calling us fools?" Garrett asked, his temper starting to seep into his tone.

"No," Thraz replied. "Your intelligence is satisfactory. It's your powers of observation which need work."

"Observation?" Anise asked.

"Until I led you to it, none of you realized the Shifter's weakness. None of you thought about the cloak disappearing when your attacks finally worked. You would go out again and face the same peril, ill-equipped."

"There are better weapons?" Garrett asked perking up.

"Sharpen your mind, not just your sword," Thraz snapped.

"Sharpen our minds?" Roven repeated.

Thraz mumbled something. "As a trader, I'm certain you can understand. Each person you deal with has weaknesses when you negotiate a price, right?"

"Well yeah," Roven said. "If you notice their crop is starting to wilt you know they want to sell quickly. Or, if their stomach is grumbling you know they haven't eaten recently and want to make a deal quickly for coin to get a meal. In both those situations, you can drive a price down."

Thraz raised his hand to silence Roven. "That's the key. What do you see? What clues are there? Roven, Anise, you two need to watch for these clues."

Garrett scowled and sprang forward. "What about me? Are you saying I'm not smart enough to see these clues?"

Thraz stood, he took a step and was within mere inches of Garrett. "You're close to the enemy, you may miss things." Thraz made a fist. "Anise and Roven support your style by being farther back. They see more of the scene than you do." Thraz punched Garrett in the stomach.

Garrett coughed and shoved Thraz back. "What was that for?"

"Demonstration," Thraz said. "Anise and Roven could see the fist I made, they could see me move my arm back to prepare, they could have read the signs and warned you. Remember what I said before the loyalty test about their talents being useful? That was a demonstration."

"Could have used a fake punch," Garrett grumbled, sitting back down.

"Needed to make a point," Thraz replied. "You're so consumed with being the best, you need to know you can't hunt alone."

"I want to destroy those things," Garrett growled. "Every one of them."

Anise locked eyes with Garrett. "We can hunt, we can destroy, but even we need support."

"And you need to be binding souls," Thraz added. "Did you hear my talk with the others? We aren't some altruistic group of angels out to do good here. Your job is to make sure the Touched don't taint souls so they're useful for us."

"Those glyphs are a waste of my time," Garrett protested. "I'm a soldier, not a bargain dealer, or an evidence destroyer. Release glyphs, soul binding, demonic pacts, they have no appeal for me."

"What about your patron?" Thraz questioned. "Your father, Azazel, is a fallen angel turned fury. He bestows power upon you. He grants your strength. Your job is to use that gift of strength for his purposes. That's your deal with the Devil, or demon in this case."

"Can't there just be some other Infernals striking bargains?" Garrett asked. "That way I can focus on the hunt."

"Think about that," Thraz said. "Some human is under attack. You save him, then another Infernal arrives after you leave to offer safety and protection? These people are vulnerable at the moment of danger. That's the best time. That's why you need to comply."

Garrett grumbled again. He got up and started walking away.

"We aren't finished," Thraz called after him.

Garrett kept walking. He went to the door and left. Anise sprang up from her seat. "I better follow him."

"I'm coming too," Roven said. He stood but stopped to look at Thraz for approval. Thraz nodded and Roven skipped to catch Anise. They headed out after Garrett.

Outside there was no sign of Garrett. Anise stopped and put her hand to her chest. Roven stood silently, waiting for instruction. Anise rotated her body slowly. After she turned a full circle, she stopped. "I can't track him in any direction."

"What can we do then?" Roven asked. "If we can't track him how do we follow? We may not have an option but to wait."

Anise's face scrunched. "Wait?"

"When I was a trader, we would get people who were angered during bartering," Roven said. "Sometimes instead of pressing for a deal, you're better to let the person walk away. Oftentimes they return calmer and you get a better price for your wares. Maybe Garrett wishes time alone to calm down."

Anise let out a sigh, gazing longingly down the street as though watching. "He's never stormed off like that. Where would he go? What will he do?"

"What did he do before he was summoned?" Roven asked. "His old life may be the answer."

"I don't know what he did," Anise said. "I never asked. We don't talk about our old lives much. I guess we have our reasons."

"Reasons?"

"Not the time for such discussions," Anise replied. "If anyone will know it'll be Thraz."

They returned inside. Thraz made his rounds between groups of Infernals training. He was quiet but made disapproving gestures and facial expressions. A few times he forcefully adjusted individuals' arms or weapons to the correct position. He kicked their ankles and shins to correct errors in footing and stance.

"He doesn't seem happy," Roven observed.

"Is he ever?" Anise replied. "He lost his temper with me before I even knew his name; although I did stab him."

"You what?" Roven asked.

"I woke from the trance alone in a room. I heard footsteps. I hid behind the door and I had my dagger. When he came in, I stabbed him hoping to flee."

"That's lucky," Roven said. "I was terrified. I thought I'd wronged someone with connections. I thought those tales of secret organizations were true. I thought I was going to be tortured or murdered. I almost cried."

Thraz bobbed his head when he spotted Anise and Roven. He walked over. "Any idea where he went?"

"None," Anise replied. "I can't even track him."

"I had thought..." Roven began in a sheepish tone.

"Yes?" Thraz replied. "you had thought what?"

"If he was running, he might run to something from his past life. What did he do before he came here?"

"Soldier," Thraz replied. "Was handy with a bayonet on his rifle. That's why he favours the spear."

"What about the armour?" Anise asked.

Thraz chuckled. "He thought if he was going to be a soldier with a spear, he should have an appropriate uniform. I found him some old armour. He can't resume that life though."

"Why not?" Roven asked.

"He's been away. He disappeared without permission. They would label him a deserter and execute him," Thraz replied. "As soon as he was tapped, returning to that part of his life became a death sentence."

"Must be confusing," Roven said. "Is there another clutch nearby he could go to? Somewhere to seek refuge?"

Thraz shook his head. "Nearest clutch is almost four days walk. Even if he tried to fly, it would be two days. He couldn't fly in broad daylight; would attract too much attention."

"We can't track him, he has no past life to go to, no nearby clutch..." Anise listed her thoughts aloud. "Did he have a home?"

"Barracks," replied Thraz

"A family?" Anise asked.

"Azazel. His mother left him at an orphanage," Thraz said.

"Would he go there?" Roven asked.

Thrax shook his head and let out a laugh. "Hated it. Doubt he would feel any reason to return. In many ways, Anise, you and Garrett have very similar stories. What would he do there? Seek employment?"

Anise drew her dagger, stomped over to a nearby shipping crate, and stabbed at it repeatedly. "This is so frustrating! Why can't we figure out how to find him? I couldn't even sense his aura anymore." As she finished a tear rolled down her cheek. "He's been there whenever I needed him. He saved me, watched over me, protected me..." she sniffed and wiped the tear. "And when he needs me, where am I? Here. What am I doing for him? Nothing. I feel so useless." She stabbed the crate again, dropped to her knees, and let out a growl. She sat with her arm and head resting on the crate.

Thraz and Roven walked over. They stood beside her. Most of the Infernals in the room heard her outburst and were looking on with concerned expressions.

"Our only option may be to wait for his return," Roven said.

"He's always come back before," Thraz said.

"Before?" Anise asked.

"He hasn't run out like this in some time," Thraz said. "But he always came back."

"This happened before?" Anise repeated.

"A few times, when he first arrived," Thraz replied. "He didn't want to believe what he was. Thought he was hallucinating. Thought he was drunk once or twice. He had some denial. But every time he ran out unsure of who or what he was, he always came back."

Anise sighed. "I don't like this. I'm going to search for him." She picked herself up and went to the door.

As she walked out she heard Thraz's instruction. "One quick patrol, bring him back if you find him. If you don't find him soon, return so you can get some rest."

Anise waved her arm in acknowledgement. She walked out of the warehouse snapping the door shut forcefully behind her.

Chapter 8 - Compassion

hraz stood before the clutch. The last few Infernals rushed to assemble as he began. "There is still the need to remember the soul-binding glyph," he said while holding up a glyph torch. "This is essential for our recruiting. It is necessary because those bound souls fuel our DHEC. There is no way to overemphasize the importance of this action."

Anise stared blankly. Her head tilted sideways.

"Are you alright?" Roven whispered. "You look distracted."

Anise blinked and looked at Roven. "It's been almost three days since Garrett ran out. I'm so worried I can barely concentrate and Thraz is so strongly focused on this glyph. How does he do it?"

"It must be hard for him too," Roven replied. "Garrett was the unofficial second in command around here. Now I guess that honour is yours."

"Don't even think that," Anise hissed. "He'll be back. I know he will."

"He has no home, and can't return to anywhere. Where would he spend three days?"

"He's resourceful and strong. He probably stayed in an abandoned house. Could have found an old bed and blanket."

Roven surveyed the room. "Who do you think our temporary teammate will be?"

Anise gave him a mild slap on the arm. "I'm not replacing him."

Roven rubbed his arm. "I said temporary." He pouted and his focus returned to Thraz's speech.

Thraz finished with another demonstration of the soul-binding glyph. He made the infinity symbol, the unending circle, and the swirl around infinity five times. Thraz stepped down from his crate and strolled through the training area. He casually watched as the Infernals paired off and sparred. After his speech, Thraz took on a more mellow tone. He observed but he wasn't actively correcting mistakes.

"He must be worried too," Roven said as he and Anise prepared to spar with their aura weapons. "He has no focus. Those mistakes are things he always scolds us for."

Anise nodded in agreement. "Even his soul-binding glyph speech was less enthusiastic than normal."

"He forgot to mention the release glyph for defeated Touched too," Roven commented.

They faced off and exchanged weapon strikes. Anise used her whip to lash at Roven. He practiced spinning his chains in circles forming the equivalent of a large disc to block with. He shot the chain straight out to parry and redirect Anise's attacks. Roven flicked his arm and sent his chain at Anise. She dodged. Roven jerked his arm, a ripple went through the chain and it redirected. The chain wrapped around Anise.

"You're getting better at that," Anise said. "Soon you'll be using the initial attack as a feint and the redirect as the real attack."

Roven nodded in agreement, dismissing the chain. "Take your dagger out and charge me as a melee fighter would. I want to see if I can wrap you up from behind."

Anise dismissed her aura whip and drew her dagger. She held it up like an opponent would hold a larger sword. "Ready."

Roven's arm shot forward and the chain sailed straight at Anise, she swung the dagger, easily deflecting the chain. Anise sprinted toward Roven, he quickly tugged the chain and had it return. The chain wrapped around Anise's ankles, dragging her to the ground. Her dagger was only inches from scratching Roven's leg.

"You need to be faster," Anise said. "You've got the technique, but if I were faster and holding a longer weapon you'd be injured."

Roven released the chain and allowed his aura to subside. "The flick back, it still takes me too long. I want to make sure the target is charging me so their focus isn't on my chain. Should I try to strike from away or skip backward for more time?"

Anise nodded. "Try it. We can try the skip or jump back, or even dart side to side. Once an enemy is in close, you'll need to be able to fight." She took a few steps back and readied her dagger.

Roven forced his arm forward. The chain shot straight through the air. Anise easily deflected the diversionary attack and charged in. Roven darted to his left and pulled the chain. The chain sped back, closing behind Anise unseen. Roven took a few steps back as the gap between he and Anise narrowed. His chain wrapped around Anise's body when she was still several paces away.

"Good," Anise said. "Chain in your right, run left, the enemy won't see it coming. Adding distance made a difference."

"It's good because the chain moved faster than you did," Roven replied. "You're not as focused as usual."

"I know," Anise grumbled.

"Can we try again?" Roven asked. "The training might help you too. Come at me."

Anise plodded back to her start position and readied her dagger. She gave a wave and Roven flung his chain. Anise had a blank look on her face, then a flash of concern; she raised her dagger at the last moment and was sent to the ground by Roven's chain.

"Sorry," Roven said. "I thought the wave meant you were ready."

Anise stood and readied herself. "Go."

Roven sent his chain again. Anise deflected and jogged toward Roven. He pulled the chain back and easily wrapped her up.

"I feel confident about this with Shamblers," Roven said releasing his aura. "I'm worried about those Shifters though."

Anise picked herself up and put her dagger away. "Speed doesn't seem to matter with them, timing does. We need two things to fight those creatures: someone as a target, and a way to save the target." Her voice trailed off as she finished speaking. She lowered her hands to her side and stared off into space. Gazing at the sky through one of the warehouse windows, Anise was a statue.

Roven walked over and stood beside her. "I know you're worried about him." He put his hand on Anise's shoulder. "Either he'll come back or we'll find him, somewhere."

Anise put her hand on Roven's; she slowly slid the hand down her arm and guided it away. "I don't want comfort, thank you." Anise trudged to one of the chambers used for sleeping and closed the door.

Thraz walked over to Roven. "What happened to her?"

"Mentioned fighting Shifters, and needing to heal whoever takes the attack from them as part of a strategy..." Roven replied.

Thraz shook his head and sighed. "I need her in the field, but she can't hunt if she's distracted."

"You're worried about Anise being a liability?" Roven asked.

"Right now it's a certainty. If she freezes up and shuts down at the mention of a Shifter's victim, what'll she do when confronted with one?"

The two stood in silence. Roven had no reply, and Thraz's decision sounded final. Roven surveyed the room. "I guess I'll need to be assigned to another team."

"I've got the new leviathan that was just tapped earlier this week. She needs to prepare before she can go out. You can spar with her for now."

"Surprising," Roven commented.

"Why are you surprised?" Thraz asked.

Roven turned his head to face Thraz. "I'm still pretty new myself. Anise is still working on training me. I'm surprised you wouldn't pair a new Infernal with someone more experienced."

"Don't belittle your own abilities," Thraz barked. Placing his hand on Roven's shoulder, his tone changed to one of assurance. "You're able to catch Anise. Leviathans use transformation fighting like imps do, so you're useful there. Leviathans are essentially large serpents; many use aura tendrils similar to your chains. Try working with her."

"I appreciate your confidence," Roven said. "I'll try not to disappoint you."

Thraz waved to a young woman standing off in the corner. "Calypso, come over here."

She turned. As she spun her black hair swung around her waist. Her shimmering blue eyes narrowed as her gaze locked on Roven. Slowly, she strutted across the room.

Roven extended his hand. "I'm Roven."

She shook his hand. "I know who you are." She then glared at Thraz. "I'm to work with this imp then?"

"He's a mid-range fighter," Thraz said. "You'll be well suited to pair off for now."

Calypso sighed. She closed her eyes, her stone was on a headband and it shone royal blue. Her aura surrounded her. A massive serpent's tail formed. She twisted. The tail crashed into Roven's body sending him to the ground.

"That was a cheap shot!" Roven yelled, springing to his feet.

Calypso stood still and straight-faced. "Aura manifestation means aura utilization. You should have anticipated my attack."

"We weren't even preparing to spar," Roven argued.

"Thraz said we were paired up."

"A little warning would have been nice."

"Touched don't warn, they attack."

"Enough!" Thraz bellowed. "Take that energy, that rage, and that frustration and use them for training. You're working together, figure it out."

Thraz walked away as Roven and Calypso locked eyes with one another. Roven hummed, his aura surrounding him. He flicked his arm and chains ran through the air. Calypso used her aura tail to intercept the chain. When her tail was wrapped by Roven's chains, she dismissed it. The chains clattered as they hit the stone floor. Calypso thrust her arm forward. An aura tail manifested from her hand, it came forward and sent Roven sprawling back. Roven growled. His aura flashed, then he was gone.

Calypso chuckled. "He's running away from a training exercise? Such a contemptible display."

As she finished speaking Roven struck. With a small rubber strap in his hand, he struck Calypso in the back of the head; she fell to the floor.

"What was that?" she asked, picking herself off the floor.

"Imp camouflage," Roven replied. "I'm still working on developing the technique, but it helps with my infiltration missions. Your ability to use your aura tail from your hand is impressive."

"It is," she replied smugly.

The two continued to set themselves against each other. Roven used his camouflage a second time. Calypso responded with several aura tails from various parts of her body; the tails acted like a protective sphere around her. Roven tried using his chains, but they were deflected. Calypso struck out but missed.

They continued to the point of mutual exhaustion. Roven thrust forward to attack and whirled his chain to defend. Calypso stood still for most of the training allowing her aura to do the work. When their auras finally collapsed they were both hunched forward with their hands on their knees, panting deeply and sweating profusely.

"I think...I think we did, alright," Roven gasped out.

Calypso nodded. "You're better than I expected."

They staggered to some shipping crates and sat down. Calypso was able to sit fairly quickly, Roven used his arms for support and eased himself down slowly, his face wrenched from time to time as he positioned himself.

Roven glared at Calypso. "How? How can you be so good and so arrogant when you're as new as you are?"

"Your perception of arrogance stems from my past," Calypso said. "Unlike most of the wretches here, I had a noble upbringing. I have an education, refinement, and now I live in a warehouse. Pardon me if I seem arrogant, pretentious, or otherwise unpleasant. This is not a life I was prepared for, nor is it one I wish to accept."

Shock filled Roven's face. He stared blankly. His face flushed slightly. "Sorry, I didn't know. You've walked away from more than most of us."

"I WAS TORN AWAY!" She shouted. "How could I expect some peasant to realize the impact this has?"

Roven's eyes flashed for a moment, he leaned forward on his crate. "Peasant, I was a trader, a merchant. Now I get looked down on and called 'Imp'."

"You've gone from one life of servitude to another. How can you even begin to compare to me and to what I've lost?"

Roven bit his lower lip, silent for a moment before speaking. "I had contacts, contracts, a life of freedom and what seemed like endless possibility. Every day I sought out opportunities to better my station in life. I was moving up. I was making gains, gains that would have left me comfortable in my older years.

Now...now I'm degradingly called 'Imp'. Maybe it's not as large as your loss, but it was my whole world too."

"My apologies," Calypso said. "I assumed you were a farmer, or maybe one of these new factory workers."

"Surprisingly, a lot of our clutch members are," Roven said. "I thought about it earlier. Demons are opportunistic and look for individual gains, so why breed with farmers and serfs? Why wouldn't they have worked their way into the higher parts of society?"

Calypso paused, her eyes darted about. She chewed her lip lightly. "Social barriers I suppose."

"What do you mean?"

"In the past a high social standing was familial. Newcomers were seldom accepted. Entry would have been quite difficult. However, whores and peasants have little suspicion of newcomers. That suspicion seems to diminish when a few coins are involved."

Roven rolled his eyes. "I'll try to minimize my offence from your statement," he replied with a hint of sarcasm.

Calypso chuckled.

"What's so funny?" Roven asked.

"I couldn't stop myself. Your unique style of cloaked aggression is amusing at times."

"Cloaked aggression?" Roven repeated.

"Trying that humorous tone to veil how offended you were by my comment."

Anise emerged from her room. She had removed her trademark dress and was now wearing black pants and a deep purple blouse with a black knee-length coat. She marched over to Roven and Calypso.

"I communed, meditated, and chanted. I finally found a trace of him. Assemble your gear, we can go get him."

Roven sprang up. "Excellent. We've just done some sparring, had a brief rest we're ready to go."

Calypso stood slowly and extended her hand. "I'm new, call me Calypso."

Roven's head bounced back and forth. "Where are my manners? Anise this is Calypso, she's a leviathan, and she's strong. Calypso this is..."

Calypso cut him off. "Anise, the succubus. One of two fully developed Infernals in this clutch."

Anise's eyes widened with surprise, her head tilted slightly. "I'm known to someone as green as you. I'm honoured."

"Your name is on many lips in this clutch," Calypso replied. "You and Garrett Ladd. You're revered by some and envied by others."

Anise smirked. "Which category do you belong to?"

Calypso smirked in response. "My thoughts are yet to be decided."

Roven burst back into the conversation. "You said you were able to sense Garrett's aura, Anise?"

Anise disengaged from Calypso. "Yes, Roven, I managed to get a glimpse of him. We should go; it's faint and I don't want to lose it."

Anise, Roven, and Calypso headed for the door. They were almost across the practice room when Thraz appeared, blocking the door. "Where are you going?" he asked.

"I found a trace of Garrett. We're going to retrieve him," Anise said.

Thraz stared into her eyes. "That look, that unwavering conviction. You'll go no matter what I say. The three of you go, bring him back."

Anise scurried past Thraz and out the door. Roven and Calypso jogged to catch her. They went out into the Old Quarter.

Anise pointed down the road, deeper into the Old Quarter. "He's down that way."

She darted down the road. Roven and Calypso ran to catch up. After a few blocks, Anise stopped. The others stopped just behind her.

"What is it?" Roven asked.

Anise closed her eyes and was silent.

"What's happening?" Calypso asked.

Roven put his fingers to his lips. "Shhhh." He put his finger down and whispered, "she's tracking him through his aura. She needs to concentrate."

Anise rotated slowly, her eyelids fluttered as she turned. Her eyelid movements became more rapid and she stopped. "This way!"

They rushed down the street with no activity around. No lights from candles or hearth fires lit any window or doorway. With the sun setting, this area would soon have only the light of the moon and stars. There were no lights installed in this older area among the abandoned and dilapidated homes.

Anise stopped in front of a building, larger than most, with a faint light coming from inside. "In here."

Roven pulled out a glyph torch. "Before we go in we should use illusion glyphs to change our appearance. You don't look like you belong."

With a nod, Anise gave her permission. Roven focused his energy into the small rod; it glowed. He traced the shape of an eye, and then a wavy cloud-shaped bubble around it. Anise shimmered and appeared to be wearing her dress. Roven used the same glyph on Calypso to alter her appearance for the humans in the building.

"What about you?" Calypso asked.

"My clothes are from my prior life," Roven replied. "I look like an average trader."

Slowly, Anise opened the door and walked in. Roven and Calypso followed. There were a few lit candles and a small fire in the hearth. This was no tavern. The tables were in one long row near the hearth, the rest of the floor space was open, with blankets laid out. There were scrawny children focused on the door, some hiding behind a chair or under a blanket.

"This isn't a place for you," a voice said from the far end of the room. "There's nobody here to pay for those ladies' services. I suggest you take your trade elsewhere."

"We're looking for a friend," Anise said. "He..."

"I told you we don't have your kind of friend here," the voice interrupted.

Roven stepped forward and shielded his eyes trying to see through the glow of the candles, to see the figure attached to this voice. "She doesn't mean a friend for just this evening. A real friend of ours has gone missing in this area. We are concerned for his well-being, and we want to find him. Has a man come through here recently?"

"Nobody has come today, just we who were already here," the voice replied.

Calypso and Roven turned to leave, but Anise stepped forward. "He's been missing three days. Has anyone come here in the past three days?"

Silence.

Anise repeated herself. "Has anyone come here in the past three days?"

Silence.

Anise looked around at the children's faces, many were stricken with fear. Some of the children shook, hunkering down to remain hidden. "Garrett!" she yelled. "Are you here?"

Garrett's voice responded. "It took you three days to track me?"

"You didn't make it easy for us," Anise said. "What is this place?"

"An alternative," Garrett replied. He stepped out into the light. "It's alright, children. They're not here to cause harm to any of us. They were worried about my safety."

With his words, the panic and fear in most of the faces around the room faded. Some children continued clinging to objects and keeping partly behind them, cautiously observing.

"An alternative to what?" Calypso asked.

Garrett's eyes met Calypso's. "Who are you?"

"She's new," Roven answered. "Calypso, meet Garrett. Garrett, this is Calypso."

"Now that the introductions are done, may I have my answer?" Calypso asked.

"An alternative to an orphanage," the voice from before said. A man stepped out into the light. He was thin, his ribs visible on his sides, seen through the tears of his shirt. His pants were worn through and patched.

"What kind of alternative?" Anise asked.

Garrett spoke up. "The kids come here, they go out and beg, look for errands or day labour. When they get food or coins they bring them back. They support one another, like the family they never had."

Calypso's arms crossed and her brow furrowed as she surveyed the room. "What work is there for such children?"

The man answered. "They sweep shops, tidy shelves, clean pans for the baker, wrap meat for the butcher and clean the shop, unload carts for farmers and merchants, whatever someone is willing to pay or trade for."

"Must be terrible," Roven commented.

"No," Anise said with her eyes starting to water. "This is a better alternative. Better than older kids taking what little you have. Better than administrators beating whoever the felt like, for whatever reason or no reason. This, this may not look it, but it's better."

"Garrett, who is this man?" Roven asked.

"We grew up together," Garrett answered. "He was like a brother to me. He got a factory job but was injured by a machine. He lost his left hand. Now he's a beggar again, helping the next generation."

"These children appear malnourished," Calypso observed. "Wouldn't they benefit from the meals provided at a proper facility?"

Many of the children slunk away from Calypso, concealed more by their hiding places. The one-handed man looked at her with hurt in his eyes. "You can't imagine. There they get fed, but they're mistreated. Here we work for our supper, we share what we have, and we manage to be happier than Garrett and I ever were. I'm even teaching them to read."

"John was always there for me as a child," Garrett said. "He saw something in me and nurtured it. Because of him making sure I ate and I was strong, I was able to make it as a soldier."

"And now look at you," John chuckled. "On some special, plain clothing, assignment. Trying to pass yourself off as a beggar for whatever reason."

Anise raised an eyebrow. "He knows about our work?"

"I told him I do special assignments," Garrett replied. "I said our usual base was unfit for a short time. I've been granted refuge here."

Anise reached into her pocket. She pulled out a small cloth sack with a drawstring. "I'm sure we owe them something for their support. This purse should be sufficient." She lightly tossed the purse to John.

John fumbled the one-handed catch. He used his hand and teeth to pull the drawstring and open the top of the sack. His face beamed with joy at the sight of the coins inside. "Thank you. Thank you so much. Our doors are open to you if you need a place to stay again."

Garrett nodded. "Thank you, my brother. Our base should be fine now, but we will remember your kindness."

Garrett picked up his spear and fastened it to his back. He walked out without another word. Anise, Roven, and Calypso silently followed. They went through the streets of the Old Quarter back to the warehouse.

Chapter 9 – Teaching

"Formation training?" Garrett groaned.

"Yes," Thraz replied. "With Calypso joining you, there needs to be four-man cohesion instead of just a partnership."

"Aren't they still just backing me up?" Garrett asked. "I'm meant for heavy combat, the others are my support."

"I beg your pardon!" Calypso snapped. "I can handle myself in the heat of a fight. I don't need your protection."

Garrett stood silent for a moment. He manifested a wing and swiped it at Calypso. She tumbled to the ground.

Calypso picked herself up. "A warning would have been nice."

"Touched don't warn, they attack." Roven blurted out followed by an uncharacteristically smug chuckle.

Calypso locked her eyes on Roven as she got to her feet. "Well placed, you annoying little imp." She smiled slightly as she finished saying imp.

Roven's mouth flattened. His eyes narrowed.

"Have I bested your repertoire of comments already?" Calypso jeered as she stood up.

Roven stood silent. His lips quivered. He blinked repeatedly.

"Searching for words?" Calypso prodded.

Roven wiped a bead of sweat from his forehead. "I said all I needed to say."

Calypso roared with laughter. "What kind of merchant must you have been being so inept at discourse?"

"Enough!" Garrett shouted at Calypso. "You still have much to prove." His gaze floated to Roven. "Both of you."

Without looking at Garrett, Calypso extended an aura tail toward him. Garrett manifested his other wing, wrapping the pair around his body as a shield. Calypso extended three more tendrils and battered Garrett's wings. He stood strong. Drawing his spear, he extended it. Garrett allowed his aura to flow through the spear. He shrugged his wings aside and began deflecting the aura tails with his spear. The aura on aura crashes sent ripples of energy through the room.

"Aren't you going to fight back?" Calypso demanded.

Garrett stood, feet planted firmly as Calypso pressed the attack. Garrett remained stationary. He intercepted and handled every strike masterfully. With each passing strike, Calypso's lips curled in a snarl. Her fists clenched.

Each deflected strike caused Calypso's eyes to narrow. Glaring at Garrett, she intensified her demonic energy. With her aura swelling around her, Calypso's eyes flashed open and her snarl widened exposing her grinding teeth. Garrett maintained an emotionless demeanour; his eyes tracked Calypso's attacks. As he tracked each attack, he deflected it and anticipated the next. His aura maintained an unwavering balance throughout the exchange.

Calypso's increased strength turned the ripples of energy bursting from her attacks into waves. The waves ran through the entire training room, knocking down the nearby training dummies. As dummies and barrels fell, the waves pushed the other Infernals, drawing them to the spectacle. Thraz observed from afar as the two battled.

"Thraz, what will you do?" a voice asked from within the crowd of Infernals.

"They need to sort this out themselves," Thraz answered, folding his arms.

Calypso continued a four-tailed onslaught and Garrett stood motionless, easily stopping or redirecting every strike with his spear and wings. The intensity of the battle mesmerized the motionless crowd of Infernals. Sweat poured down Calypso's face. Her strikes slowed from lashes to lunges. She heaved her body and arms as she struck forward. Garrett preserved his calm disposition. He easily intercepted the awkward movements and strikes; his wings at his sides and deflecting the incoming tails with only his spear.

"Focus," Garrett commanded. "You must have complete control of your aura."

"Don't patronize me," Calypso roared. "Feel my power." She swung her arms launching a two-tailed attack.

Garrett continued his emotionless defence. He parried each laboured strike as Calypso pitched her tentacles at him. A few beads of sweat emerged on his forehead. The defence was methodical. He maintained a steady pace with his breath, his eyes tracking Calypso's attacks, his spear moved simply with no wasted effort.

Enthralled by the sight before them; the entire clutch gathered like the crowds watching two gladiators battle. Garrett in his ancient armour stood ready to please the crowds of the Colosseum of Rome itself.

The crowd murmured as the battle waged on. Despite the voices intermingling into white noise, Anise heard a few of the remarks.

"Why hasn't Garrett attacked?" one voice said.

"How does Calypso have that much stamina?" another questioned.

"I hope I can be that strong one day," someone said.

Anise stood by but her look of concern faded. Roven noticed. "You don't look very concerned."

Anise calmly continued watching the match. "I've sparred with Garrett. He knows how to handle my whip, these leviathan tentacles are similar weapons."

"She doesn't try to wrap an enemy," Roven observed. "She's attacking in a one-dimensional manner. Her moves are inexperienced and easy for Garrett to read."

Anise nodded. "Mmhmm." Her eyelids fluttered and she began to glow. "Her DHEC control is faltering. She won't be able to maintain her aura much longer. The waves of energy she emits are weakening. Can't you feel it?"

Roven closed his eyes. A mild aura glow surrounded him. "I can't sense the aura the way you can. I do feel less force coming from her blows though. She's tiring."

Anise smirked. "Tiring? She's exhausted. She's continuing on rage and frustration."

Roven's eyes widened slightly as he inspected Calypso. Sweat poured down her face, and dripped from her nose and chin. Her chest heaved as she inhaled and exhaled; her breathing audible even with the noise from the aura-on-aura collisions. Calypso widened her stance. Her knees trembled. Her arms quaked. She reduced her attack from four aura tentacles to two.

Calypso dropped to one knee. Another aura tail faded to nothing. Her last aura tail remained manifested, but it barely moved. With a gasp, she lunged it straight at Garrett again. No ploys, no deception, a head-on frontal assault. He masterfully knocked it away with his spear. Calypso fell to the ground, her aura faded away. She lost consciousness.

Garrett released his aura. "DHEC conservation," he addressed the room, "is crucial. You cannot channel more energy than you can handle in an attempt to scare or intimidate a foe. Our bodies can only handle so much demonic power before we are overwhelmed. If you can't manage your emotions and energy you end up unconscious." He pointed at Calypso. "She put on an amazing show. You could all learn from her power, but learn better control."

After the address, Garrett watched the Infernals nod and whisper amongst themselves. Many nodded and used hand gestures but the sounds flowed together in a muffled hum of generic noise combining discussion and reflection on the lesson Garrett presented.

With a smirk, Thraz patted Garrett's shoulder. Thraz raised his head to address the crowd. "Learn from this. You may face one Touched, you may face four.

What will keep you alive is your ability. Control the DHEC. Control yourselves. Control the humans' fears so you can mark them. Control the situation."

Calypso moaned and struggled to sit up. Roven tried to assist, but she shook him off. She sat, defeated. She didn't speak, she didn't try to stand. She simply sat with a look of shame on her face.

Garrett turned his gaze toward Calypso. "That was an impressive show of strength. Rest up, you'll need to recover before we go hunting." He grinned.

Calypso's eyes glinted. She smiled, "I'll take my leave now."

Anise and Roven shared a subtle smirk. "Still trying to use her upbringing to elevate herself," Roven whispered.

Anise nodded. "I believe they call it saving face. Garrett provided her an opportunity to avoid the shame, she's accepting it."

"Nice of him," Roven said. "I'm not sure I'd do the same."

"Garrett was a soldier," Thraz said coming up behind them. "He may have grown up in the streets, but he does understand pride."

Thraz walked away, he waved his arms dismissing the Infernals back to their training. He sent two squads of four out on patrols. Calypso struggled to stand. She used a fallen barrel for assistance. Once upright, she staggered to the nearest crate and sat down. Every time her feet left the ground she panted. She shook with each step.

Anise walked over. "He's good."

"Better...better than I...expected," Calypso forced between heaving breaths.

"Don't feel too bad," Anise continued, placing a hand on Calypso's shoulder. "He's got more experience with his aura and in actual battle than anyone else here."

Calypso shrugged Anise's hand away, the motion almost caused her to fall over. "I don't require or desire your comfort or your pity. Give me a moment and I'll be off to take my rest."

"I have no desire to comfort you. As for pity, you're not worth the effort." Anise stood up. She walked over to where Roven stood. Garrett was in the training area. He straightened target dummies and offered assistance to other Infernals.

"I suppose we should make some rounds and help out," Anise said cheerfully.

"Until Calypso recovers our new team won't be deployed," Roven replied. "We can help now and hunt later."

Anise and Roven went around the room. They corrected other Infernals stances and techniques, helped with focus and DHEC channelling, and provided a few demonstrations where needed.

Chapter 10 – Exposure

Calypso emerged from a side room beaming with energy. Wielding two rectangular hammerheads on shafts, she smashed a training dummy. The heads were square at the ends and roughly three times as long as they were high and wide, each with a cone-shaped spike at the top.

Roven walked over. "What are those?"

"Mauls," Calypso replied.

"Interesting choice for someone with a greater upbringing," Roven probed. "Any reason you have such weapons?"

"I learned to duel with skinny swords. Fancy, upscale, but too dainty," Calypso grinned. "These twin hammers flow through the air nicer, and they make an impact."

"Aren't they harder to control?" Anise asked from behind her.

Calypso spun around. The mauls swirled through the air. Her motions were far more graceful and fluid than the aura tail strikes she launched at Garrett. "I've worked to turn something blunt into something graceful. Hammer dance instead of sword dance. It delighted some as a novelty and met opposition from others."

"That doesn't answer the matter of control," Anise said.

Calypso swirled around. The maul flowed through the air. She twirled the handles and performed an elegant dance. Suddenly, she stopped. The maul heads were mere inches from Anise and Roven's faces. "How is that for control?"

"Shocking," Roven said.

"Surprising and fortunate at the same time," Anise said as she pushed the maul to the side.

"It's getting dark," Thraz said as he and Garrett joined the three. "I need to send you out. The patrols from this morning aren't back yet. They were supposed to be on a short-range route. Should be back by now."

"I'll lead, Anise and Calypso in the middle, Roven bring up the rear," Garrett ordered.

"Why?" Calypso challenged, gearing up for an argument.

"I'm the team lead, I take the front position," Garrett said. "Anise is in the middle for ranged support with her whip. Roven is in the rear because he's good at watching for pursuers. You're walking third to be able to put power to the rear if needed quickly, and you can move past Anise to aid me with relative ease too."

"Oh...I suppose that makes sense," Calypso replied. She fell in line and followed Anise out the door.

As they walked through the streets Garrett spent more time checking alleyways than usual. He picked up larger pieces of debris and garbage, opened doors, and looked in windows.

"What's he doing?" Calypso whispered.

"Looking for anything," Anise replied. "Signs of a skirmish, blood, bodies, damage to the area from aura weapons. He's concerned about our missing patrols. Any indication of where they were and what transpired is important."

Calypso and Roven scampered into the alley with Garrett. Anise stood watch at the street, her head switching from side to side.

Garrett dug through pile after pile of refuse. Throwing the last few pieces of debris aside, he huffed in frustration. "Do you sense any auras, Anise?"

"Nothing beyond our own," she replied. "I'm trying to search for even a trace, a disturbance, anything. It's as though they were wiped from existence without a trace."

Head slightly down, Garrett trudged toward the street. "We should move on then."

Anise and Calypso walked beside one another. Roven brought up the rear. The next alley was very short and empty. There was little to look through. The alley after that was a mess. There were old boards from houses, old doors, garbage containers neglected by town sanitation workers, and a putrid stench assaulting the senses more than most alleys in the Old Quarter. Anise took up her sentry position and channelled DHEC energy, hoping to detect a faint aura. Garrett started hurling the wooden boards and doors; his snarl and vigour alerted Roven to pick items at a distance. Calypso got in close. A wooden beam went sailing past her head.

"Be more careful," Calypso scolded. "You almost hit me."

Garrett scowled at her. "We are looking for friends of ours. My comrades mean something to me. We will find them. I will find out what happened. If anything or anyone hurt them, they'll answer to me."

Calypso backed away. Garrett's growling voice and snarling teeth were very pronounced. His hair was starting to take on an orange tinge and his skin colour turned slightly. Without channelling, his demon self was emerging.

"I've detected something," Anise called. "It's faint, a few blocks away. We should hurry."

Garrett sprang from the pile of refuse and charged to the edge of the alley. "Which way?"

Anise pointed. Garrett sprinted away before she could open her mouth to speak. Anise ran after him. Calypso and Roven struggled to keep pace. Garrett quickly scanned down the alleys he passed for two blocks. He stopped at the third. His aura emerged and his wings expanded fully. He stomped into the alley. Anise followed Garrett's example, her wings and whip were ready before she reached the edge of the building.

At the end of the alley, there were two bodies propped against walls and two lying on their faces. Garrett spun, there were no other bodies to be seen.

"I sense two," Anise said as she caught up. "The others must be dead."

Roven and Calypso walked into the alley.

"You two take sentry position," Garrett instructed. "Anise and I will look around. Four bodies on the ground without any signs of blood means something dangerous came through here. Stay alert."

Roven and Calypso prepared their weapons and stood at the entrance to the alley. Roven faced in, Calypso faced out. Slowly their heads panned from side to side.

"What happened?" Garrett asked a barely conscious Infernal.

"They came out of nowhere," he replied.

"Shifters?" Garrett asked.

The Infernal coughed and wheezed. "Three of them." His chest rose and fell sharply as he forced the words.

"Did you defeat them?" Anise asked as she crouched beside Garrett.

"We got all three," he affirmed. "Managed the..." he coughed, "release glyph to..." he coughed again, "to banish them." He paused and inhaled deeply, coughing violently. "It took everything we had."

"We need to get these two to Thraz," Anise said.

"Shamblers," the second Infernal coughed. "We were chasing Shamblers when the Shifters attacked."

"How many?" Garrett asked.

"Two," he replied.

Garrett stroked his chin. "I wonder if it was a coincidence, or a trap."

The Infernal tried to meet Garrett's eyes. "I don't know."

"Did they give any indication of cooperation?" Anise asked.

The Infernal shook his head from side to side.

"How long ago?" Garrett asked.

"Before dusk," the Infernal replied.

"Calypso, you and Roven take these two to Thraz," Garrett commanded. "Anise and I will go after the Shamblers."

Calypso frowned. "Why do we have to haul them back?"

"Anise and I are stronger than the two of you," Garrett barked. "That is unless you want to try proving me wrong." His gaze pierced through Calypso as he grasped his spear handle.

"Are you provoking open combat?" Anise snapped. "Garrett, settle yourself."

"So, you think I'm better as a transport than a warrior?" Calypso questioned.

"Your aura tails could carry them," Garrett answered. His tone changed from commanding to annoyance. "It's dark enough now that you can get back to the warehouse unnoticed. Roven can act as a lookout and backup if you get attacked." He waved his hand to dismiss Calypso.

Calypso manifested four tails to carry the four Infernals. She and Roven plodded back toward the warehouse. Garrett rushed out into the streets. Anise scurried to keep up. He was a block down the road before she reached him.

"Why so fast?" Anise asked. "You're usually more collected."

"John's children," Garrett replied. "They'll be returning to that old tavern any time now. They remind me of me, I don't want to see them turned."

Anise nodded and they continued to search. They slowed their pace and headed in the direction of the tavern. Scanning each alley they raced through the streets. Approaching John's tavern, they saw two Shamblers pounding on the door.

Without hesitation, Garrett sprinted toward them. He channelled his aura and manifested his wings springing into flight. Garrett changed his aura spear to a flaming sword as he flew. Reaching the tavern entrance, he swooped down. Landing and swinging his sword he cleaved the closest Shambler in half. He sprang at the second. The Shambler shuffled back, it was sliced open across the belly. The Shambler kept shuffling back as black syrup oozed from the belly wound. Lunging forward, Garrett took another swing. The sword passed through the Shambler's neck fast and clean. The severed head remained atop the body.

Anise caught up to Garrett, wings and whip ready. Garrett kicked the Shambler below the belly wound. The body and head fell to the ground, the head rolled a few feet away.

"I'll handle the release glyph," Anise said. "Keep watch for any others."

Garrett nodded and surveyed the area. His sword faded back to spear form, clenched firmly in his hands. His eyes shifted as he assessed every window, every open doorway, and every space between buildings. His chest heaved with each breath. His eyes bulged and fixated on the task with the fervour of a man possessed.

Anise drew her glyph on each body. The semicircle, the line closing it to make the shape of a door, and then the dismissing X. The Shambler bodies crumbled and faded into nothingness.

"I don't see any more of them," Garrett said, dismissing his aura.

Anise stood up. Seeing Garrett's aura fade away she allowed hers to fade away. "Should we check the tavern?"

"What are you?"

Anise and Garrett turned and saw John standing in the tavern doorway. John shivered as he stared at his friends, trembling. The club in his hand tapped the door frame with each nervous shudder coursing through his arm. Around him, the children scrambled for any cover they could find.

Garrett sighed. "It's hard to explain."

Anise motioned toward the door. "We should go inside."

His face paralyzed, John stumbled inside. Garrett grabbed Anise's arm. When she turned, he locked eyes with her. "What are you planning?"

"Demonic charm," Anise said. "Hopefully I can channel enough DHEC energy to use my compulsion on them. If I'm successful they'll believe it was a drug-induced hallucination."

"I don't want him damned," Garrett insisted. "No soul binding."

"It could protect them, but I'll respect your wishes," Anise said.

Garrett released Anise's arm. They walked in and closed the door.

"Get everyone together in the main room," Anise instructed.

John raised an eyebrow. "Why do you want everyone assembled?"

"I'd prefer we only need to explain the situation once," Garrett replied. "Many people dislike hearing this. We don't enjoy having to speak of these things. It's easier for everyone if done once with a group rather than several times with individuals."

John pointed to a couple of the older boys. They scurried off in different directions. Doors creaked open on their rusty hinges and slammed shut. Voices echoed throughout the building as the children spoke. The melding of voices left none of the sounds intelligible. Children started to trickle in, taking their seats at the main eating table. Many showed fearful expressions on their faces.

John did his best to reassure his orphans. "Everything will be alright. I trust Garrett. Whatever this is, I know he won't let harm come to us."

The children sat and quieted. Anise walked to the head of the table. She blinked her eyes, her irises turned purple. "The men who tried to attack here were not normal," she began. "They were exposed to dangerous chemicals in the factories. They were sick. They needed help. That's why we sent them away."

"We...we saw you attack them. Th...then you knelt over them and they...they disappeared," a voice stuttered from somewhere down the table. There were murmurs of agreement.

Anise tapped her fingers on the table. The clacking of her nails on the wood brought focus to her. "The chemicals which made them sick produce a slight smell.

When exposed to it, you may hallucinate. Your mind can trick you. It's a form of intoxication far more dangerous than liquor or opium."

"I didn't smell anything," another child blurted out.

"The scent is extremely faint," Anise replied, "almost undetectable for most people. Rest assured there was nothing truly abnormal here today. A couple of sick men have been taken for proper care. Your exposure is minimal enough, you can rest easy. You are safe." As Anise spoke she shifted individual focus to each child. She made eye contact and briefly sustained it with each child.

Garrett stood motionless for Anise's address. His eyes observed the room to ensure focus remained solely on Anise and her words.

"Does anyone have any questions?" Anise finished.

The orphans sat quietly, many of them had glazed eyes and blank expressions on their faces. John spoke up. "We are in no danger then?"

"Not from those men," Garrett assured him. "I recommend using caution in the Old Quarter, but you and the children already know that."

John nodded. "Thank you, Brother."

Anise and Garrett exited the tavern. They resumed their patrol through the streets and alleys. With the sun recently set, there were some streets with candles lit in their lamps while others remained dark. The lamplighter either missed several or hadn't replaced the candles. Flickering lights with uneven gaps made checking some spots more challenging. Anise and Garrett slowed their pace to compensate for the poor lighting on the darker streets. Leaving each alley, Garrett's head turned looking back toward John's tavern.

"Are you alright?" Anise asked.

Garrett stopped walking. "Just worried."

"Worried about what?" Anise asked, her head slowly scanning the area.

"John and the children," Garrett replied. "I'm hoping the charm holds. If any of the children were losing focus..." he trailed off and looked at Anise. "Sorry. I didn't mean it that way."

"What way?"

"I didn't mean to sound like there was any failing on your part."

"I've had some concerns too," Anise admitted. "I'm still working on that type of charm channelling. I've never tried it on an audience of more than one. Do I have enough power? Did I hold their focus well enough long enough? What happens if they remember the truth?"

"If we are revealed as existing in the world..." Garrett had no end for the sentence. His voice stopped. He shook his head. "I don't want to think about how the humans would react."

"The same way a crowd responds to a streetwalker," Anise said. "Either contempt or wanting some benefit."

Reluctantly, Garrett resumed moving. His feet dragged along the street. He sighed and his head pointed forward. "Come on. We can already report two Shamblers dead; let's see if we can make that number grow."

Garrett resumed his patrol pace. He checked alleys and windows quicker than Anise.

"Slow down," Anise cautioned. "I don't want to be attacked from behind."

Garrett heeded the advice and took more time inspecting the next abandoned home he came to. He crept up and checked the window. All was dark inside, no sounds or movements.

A strange voice broke the silence. "What's all this?"

Slowly, Garrett straightened his legs and cautiously turned around. Standing across the road were two soldiers from the local garrison. The soldiers slid their muskets from their marching shoulder carry to a ready position then slowly extended the barrels forward.

Slowly, Garrett raised his arms to show them his open hands. Anise stood with her arms at her sides.

"What are you doing here?" one soldier demanded.

"Looking for the thieves who stole my necklace," Anise blurted out. "Some young men, they ran up from behind, snatched my necklace and ran off. We were trying to find them so we could bring the guards directly to them."

The guards advanced. "That's not very wise," the soldier observed. "Most people come to us directly and we conduct a search."

"She had to stop me from engaging them myself," Garrett said. "This is a compromise."

Anise's irises glowed purple as she looked at the soldiers. "We were trying to be helpful. That way a search wouldn't have been difficult for you. Sorry if our actions looked suspect."

"Take more care," the soldier replied. "These areas can be dangerous. You could have chased two thieves to a den of twenty. I'm sorry for your loss, but you would be safer returning to your home."

"Come on, Dear," Anise said motioning for Garrett to join her. "These men are right. Our lives are the most important aspect of this."

Garrett curled his lip, preparing for a growl, but kept silent and traipsed over to Anise. She put her arm around his and led him away from the house.

"Do you think it worked?" she whispered.

"I hope so," Garrett replied. "Let's just keep pretending to be defeated but look happy to be alive. That's what they'll watch for if they follow us." They slowly walked away, keeping their heads down. Garrett put an arm around Anise. She stepped closer, and pulled the arm around her, hugging it.

The two soldiers stood for a moment observing Anise and Garrett walk away. They nodded at each other, shouldered their muskets, and returned to their patrol.

"Successful deception," Garrett observed. "You're good at that."

Anise smiled. "Let's get back to the clutch. Tonight has been annoying. I don't want to stay out here. We finished the job we were given."

Garrett lifted one end of his mouth and his eyes narrowed. His face returned to normal. "Very well."

"You don't sound like you're finished out here," Anise commented.

"I believe there are more Touched out here. Those soldiers left me feeling disturbed as well. I feel anxious, as though something is about to happen. I can't rationalize the feeling, it's just there..." he trailed off. He was blinking and scanning the area.

"Even though it means going backwards, I'm happy to walk past John's tavern again," Anise said. "You're concerned about them. I can sense it."

"That's impossible to deny," Garrett admitted. "He was the brother I never had. Seeing his arm lost was hard enough, but seeing Shamblers on his doorstep was an indescribable form of devastation."

Anise started back down the street. Garrett followed. They glanced down the alleys and spaces between buildings as they passed. They walked up to John's tavern and tried the door; it was barred from inside.

"Please, go away," a child's voice said from inside the door.

"Tell John it's his friend, Garrett," Garrett responded.

"We are not to open the door," another child's voice said. "We don't know what you are, but you are dangerous."

Garrett's eyes widened, he frowned, his eyes glazed over but no tear came. "Tell John he is still my brother, and I, his. Tell him I wish him no harm. I will not pressure you for his answer. Anise and I will be on our way."

Garrett marched away from the tavern. Anise scrambled to catch him.

"Charm must have failed," Anise said.

"We're exposed," Garrett said as he quick-stepped through the street. "Thraz must know immediately. If those children alert the authorities, then our patrols become more dangerous."

Anise jogged to keep pace. "Wouldn't the guards assume the children are lying? It's a far-fetched story."

As they trudged back to the warehouse the conversation turned to quiet contemplation. Their focus was no longer on patrol. They stopped checking alleys and poorly lit buildings. Their heads hung low as they walked the last few blocks. Approaching the warehouse door the question remained unasked, but they both thought it: how would Thraz react?

Chapter 11 - Envoys

Thraz hurried Anise and Garrett into one of the small rooms in the warehouse. He slammed the door behind them. Clenching and wringing his hands, Thraz paced and puffed with each exhale. "Exposed!" he screamed. "You were exposed! How could you be so careless?"

"There were Shamblers advancing on humans," Garrett said. "I engaged them to save the humans from being turned."

"What of the soul-binding glyph?" Thraz questioned. "That should have kept them from realizing what you truly are."

Garrett's eyes went down, away from Thraz. "I couldn't mark them," he mumbled.

Thraz's eyes widened. His nostrils flared. "I beg your pardon! Why couldn't you mark them? There were two of you."

Garrett was silent.

Thraz huffed, switching from eye contact with Garrett to Anise and back. His stare conveyed more rage and frustration than words could. Tremors ran through the extremities of both causing visible rippling shakes. They gulped hard as Thraz glared through them.

"They housed Garrett," Anise replied. "The man there was like a brother to him. Our human sides and sentimentality emerge from time to time."

"Your human elements should be suppressed by now," Thraz growled. He paused for a moment; there was no reply. "I expect you two, as fully awakened Infernals, to maintain focus on the demands of your position."

Anise and Garrett exchanged glances. This felt like a headmaster's address before a caning. Sheepishly, Anise finally replied. "I suppose we're still developing in that regard."

"I regard you as leading members of this clutch," Thraz continued. "Your abilities happen to be the aspiration of many of our members. Your behaviours are emulated. Your adherence to my orders is necessary."

"Those children, I can't mark them," Garrett said. "I'll mark others we save. Those children I...I can't condemn them for eternity."

Thraz shook his head. "Personal involvement, emotional attachment, you need to disregard these and focus on the needs of your clutch, your kind."

There was a knock at the door. "Thraz, the envoy is here," one of the Infernals announced through the door.

"I'm coming," Thraz barked. "Now I have this problem. Hell has sent an envoy. In all my centuries with clutches, I have never, never, been the subject of an envoy's scrutiny." Thraz stomped out into the main room; the door slammed shut behind him.

"What's an envoy?" Anise asked.

"Demonic messenger," Garrett replied. "Most ferry messages and act as a communication method for greater demons. Aleesa, the clairvoyant you met when you first arrived, she's a special envoy who deals with unusual tasks."

"So, us not turning a few humans warrants some special demon investigator?" Anise asked.

"Depends on what the lords of Hell heard," Garrett replied.

Anise pointed at Garrett, then herself, then the door. Garrett slowly moved his head up and down, nodding in agreement. Anise opened the door. They went to join Thraz in the training room. Thraz had the training hall cleared; all the Infernals were somewhere else. Anise slowly crept through the door. Garrett followed cautiously.

"There they are," a somewhat familiar voice said.

Anise focused on Thraz; he was across the room. Standing with him was Aleesa. Aleesa motioned for Anise and Garrett to approach. They complied.

"You know why I was dispatched?" Aleesa questioned.

Garrett nodded. "We exposed ourselves while destroying some Touched. Then we tried, unsuccessfully, at convincing the people nearby they imagined the experience."

"You did more than that," Aleesa said. "Not only were you seen by the mortals, but you were seen by a small patrol of Celestials. They witnessed your abilities, then your failure. Altruistic as they are, they reported it. We heard it from an envoy from Heaven. Heaven!" Aleesa stopped. She winced at the word Heaven.

"Celestials?" Anise questioned.

"The angelic version of an Infernal," Thraz explained. "While there are those in this world who were bred by demons before being shut out of this realm, there are also those who have an angelic ancestor."

"I didn't know there were Celestials in town," Garrett commented.

"They're recent arrivals," Aleesa said. "Our sources believe they started operating here two to three weeks ago."

"What instructions have you been sent to relay?" Thraz asked. "I'm sure your orders relate to these two as much as any of my other members, or more." Thraz sounded both angry and disgusted. Anise and Garrett exchanged puzzled glances.

Aleesa blinked, then her eyes fluttered. She took a deep breath. What came out was a booming, low-pitched voice. She was just a conduit for communication. "Anise Lovejoy, Garrett Ladd, your recent actions have come to the attention of both Heaven and Hell and have been deemed unforgivable. Your powers are hereby suspended. You have no place in a demon clutch. You are hereby cast out."

Aleesa's head bobbed and shook. Her eyes blinked once, returning to normal. "Was the message clear?" she asked.

"Painfully," Thraz replied. "Anise and Garrett have been cast out from the clutch. Their access to the DHEC has been removed. They are unable to remain here any longer."

Anise and Garrett both stood frozen in place. Shivers and tremors passed through their arms and legs. Their fingers twitched. Sweat trickled down their blank faces. There were no sounds of breathing, no heaving in the chest, no movements in their throats. No sounds came from either Garrett or Anise.

"I don't sense any possession in them," Aleesa said. "Why haven't they moved? Why aren't they speaking?"

"I've only seen one Infernal be expelled from a clutch before," Thraz replied. "There was a period of such behaviour for him too. They go through a transformation when they begin to channel the DHEC. That transformation is overwhelming and usually violent. The reverse appears to be less violent but no less intense."

Thraz and Aleesa stood by as Garrett and Anise were held in their petrified state. The Infernals of the clutch emerged from the side rooms. They crept toward Thraz with puzzled expressions on their faces.

As the clutch formed a mob behind Thraz, Anise gasped. Her eyes bulged. Her chest heaved as she breathed deeply as though starved for air. "What just happened?"

"You heard the message Aleesa relayed," Thraz said. "You two have been deprived of your communion with the DHEC. There is no place for you in my clutch."

Garrett coughed violently as he regained his breath. "That's all? We're out, and that's the decree. Is there an appeal process?"

"None has ever been used," Thraz replied. "Expulsion like this is seldom used as punishment. Typically Infernals who behaved as you have are summoned to Hell and dealt with there, for eternity."

Garrett's face flashed with anger. "Where do we go?" he demanded. "I have no home, no family, I'm wanted as a deserter from the army. The only man I could trust is now terrified of me."

"Your future is no longer his concern," Aleesa calmly replied. "Thraz has his orders, and *he* knows how to obey."

Garrett lunged forward to strike Aleesa. An aura surrounded her. When Garrett punched the aura his hand bounced back and he cried out in pain.

"You no longer have your abilities," Aleesa stated. "You cannot bring harm to anyone here. You are but a mere human again."

Garrett huffed angrily as he clutched his hand. "When you summoned me, you ended the life I was living. Everything I could do as a *mere human* was taken away. I answered your call with the understanding it was permanent."

"The only permanent aspect of mortal life is death," Aleesa replied. Her facial expressions never wavered. Despite Garrett's anger, his attack, and his description of the situation she showed no emotional response.

Anise put a comforting hand on Garrett's shoulder. "My old life wasn't much better. You saw how I was cornered in that alley before you quickened. That's a constant fear for me. The protection my aura provided changed my perspective. Maybe we can manage together."

Silence took over the room. There were no answers, no murmurs. Everyone stood stunned by Anise's comment. There were no audible sounds except the shoe on floor contact as Anise and Garrett made the long trudge to the door. The crowd of Infernals stood in observance of Garrett and Anise as they made their exit.

The door closed. Garrett's head went from left to right. "Which way do we go?"

"First, we find an empty building," Anise said. "I don't care which one. There won't be any food, but we might find a usable bed."

"Second I suppose we will need to find food," Garrett said. "One nice thing about the DHEC was it sustained us. Now we have nourishment as a concern."

Anise started walking down the road toward the city itself. "How long do you suppose we have before we get hungry?"

Garrett caught up. He walked beside her. "I don't know. I don't want to think about it either, but there's no choice in the matter."

After two blocks they were in an area of the Old Quarter that had streetlights lit but many houses were dark.

"Should we split up and see which are empty?" Anise asked.

Garrett nodded. "I'll check this first one, you try the second one."

As Garrett approached the first dark house there was a crashing noise from within. He stepped back and walked briskly to Anise. "Noise from that one."

They approached the second house. There were no noises, no food smells, no scent of candles or hearth fire. The windows were dust-covered.

"This looks promising," Anise commented.

The door was ajar. Garrett pushed gently. The door opened with a creak. Garrett walked in first. "Hello?" he called. His voice echoed through the empty space.

Entering the house, they assessed its condition. The main room still had some wood for the stove; the pile was covered in cobwebs and dust.

Anise pointed at the wood. "Looks like this hasn't been disturbed in some time."

"Fortunate," Garrett replied. "We may be able to stay warm."

"I'll see if there are any blankets around," Anise said.

She walked through the house, checking for anything useful. In one room she found a broken bed frame; rough wood barely nailed together. The nails were sticking out in various ways around joints, but the wood was usable for a fire. There was no mattress or blanket. In another room, there was a lump of cloth. She inspected it to discover that it was a small pile of worn and torn blankets, far too damaged to use as anything but rags. The house had been emptied except for these items and some other garbage, nothing of worth. Anise returned to Garrett in the main room.

"There's a broken bed we can burn," Anise said. "Or we can try to barter the wood for something else."

"What would we barter for?" Garrett asked.

Anise listed items. "Food, a cooking pot, something to fetch water with."

Garrett raised his hand, causing her to pause. "Alright, how much can be salvaged?"

"The headboard and footboard are decently carved," she replied. "An extravagance by most standards. Thankfully, this was a more affluent area before the town developed and it became part of the abandoned Old Quarter. We would look like a couple down on their luck hauling the pieces to the market."

"I'm less concerned about how I look than I am about whether or not I'm recognized," Garrett said with a sigh. "The penalty for desertion is death. I can't chance being recognized. Our camouflage glyphs won't work anymore."

"Tonight we concern ourselves with warmth and sleep," Anise said. "Tomorrow, we figure out food. I wish I had the chance to retrieve my dress; there were purses in it."

"Purses?" Garrett questioned.

"I kept a few in my dress before I was summoned," Anise replied. "If a situation became too dangerous a purse could usually be used for safe passage. Keeping several meant not losing everything."

"Dangerous life on these streets," Garrett muttered as he walked to the bedroom areas.

Anise followed. "What are you doing?"

"Collecting the wood and blankets," he said. "We should collect everything while there's still some moonlight to see with."

Garrett walked into the room with the bed. He picked up the cracked frame pieces and hauled them to the main room. Pieces that were split almost through he broke over his knee, or put one end on the floor, held the other, and stomped on the break.

While Garrett dealt with the wood Anise bundled the blankets and brought them to the main room. She flung the bundled pieces out and laid them across the floor. Three blankets were worn, but usable, with minimal holes. There were two that were so badly tattered they were nothing more than rags that hadn't been split up yet.

Anise took her dagger and started slicing the rags into strips. "If we can find some oil these will be good for continued burning," she commented.

Garrett looked over. "I've got some splinters here for kindling. Don't have any flint or matches."

"I can take a strip of cloth and bring back some fire from a street lamp," Anise said. "Garrison patrols are fairly light in this area. Very few people still live here. I should be able to go unseen."

Garrett simply nodded. He resumed snapping and breaking the smaller splinters of wood for kindling.

Anise took a stick and two of the cloth rags and walked out into the street. The lit lamps revealed an empty road. The closest lit lamp stood two houses away. Anise skulked close to the buildings, checking her surroundings for people who may notice her. She approached the lamp pole and reached up. She could barely reach. The lamp reservoir was closed in. The cap was small and near the top. She looked around. She discovered a wooden box about knee height in the alley.

Anise's eyebrow raised. "A step, for now, firewood later," she commented to herself.

She brought the box and set it near the lamp post. As she lifted the lamp from its hook a puzzled look took over her face. She started scanning from the lamp to the box to the rags she had. "How do I manage all this?" she muttered to herself.

She replaced the lamp and scurried into the alley. She found three glass bottles with the tops broken. Carefully, she took them to the box. She retrieved the lamp, unscrewed the cap, and poured a small amount of oil into the two bottles with the smallest openings. She poured oil on the rags and stuffed one into the third jar. She oiled the tip of the second rag and replaced the oil cap. She tilted the lamp and opened the hatch used for lighting and extinguishing. With each task, she looked up and down the street. She dipped the oily rag into the lamp and pulled it out once lit. She dropped it in with the other rag and set the bottle down. The rags burned and the bottle shone like a lamp.

Anise put the lamp back and turned the box open end up. She placed the two bottles of oil in the box. When she reached for the flaming bottle it burned. She pulled her hand back and shook it. She managed to stifle the gasp of pain. She went to the alley and rifled through the debris. She found a broken broom handle and emerged. Checking both directions for anyone approaching, she used the broom handle as a pole. She placed the handle in the jar. Lifting the handle and jar, she created a makeshift torch. She knelt and picked the box up; tucking it under her other arm and against her hip, she scurried back to Garrett.

Anise entered the house and went straight to the hearth. She set the bottle down the best she could and used the broom handle to dig out the burning rags. Garrett had a small pile of firewood assembled. Anise moved the flaming cloth under the pile.

"What's in the box?" Garrett asked.

"Two broken wine bottles," Anise replied.

Garrett's eyes squinted together. "Broken wine bottles? What did you bring them here for?"

Anise chuckled. "They're holding more oil." She smiled as she finished speaking.

Garrett met her gaze. He smiled. "Let me guess, they were hauled here inside extra firewood."

"You're perceptive," Anise chuckled.

For the first time since their expulsion, they both smiled.

"The box might have use for hauling items later," Garrett said.

"It may," Anise admitted. "We don't have much other firewood though."

Garrett took the bottles from the box and carefully set them a safe distance from the fire. He picked up the empty box. "It seems a waste to destroy it if we don't need to."

"Set it aside then," Anise said. "Save it unless we need it."

Garrett set the box a distance from the fire. Stopping to rearrange what little wood they had he sighed and looked back. His stomach growled.

"I suppose we worry about food and money tomorrow," Anise said. Their heads dropped. Her words destroyed the few moments of joy they were sharing.

Garrett rustled the blankets he laid out on the floor by the fire. "For tonight we can sleep. Other things we can worry about tomorrow."

"If we can sleep," Anise commented. "I don't know why, but I have a strange sense that I was watched out there."

"Did you see anyone?" Garrett asked while sorting and resorting the bit of remaining firewood.

Anise walked to the window. She stayed close to the edge and looked outside. "I kept checking, but I never saw anyone, any movement, any shadows..." she trailed off looking out the window.

"Do you see something?" Garrett whispered with a concerned look on his face. His hand crept behind his back and grasped his spear.

Anise waved her arm, motioning to put the spear away. "Nothing, just a sense of...some sort of presence. I'm getting hungry. We haven't eaten in a very long time. Maybe it's some hunger-induced delusion."

Garrett pointed to the wall by the door. "I hauled the bed pieces out here. We can them it to market in the morning. I've patrolled a place or two with minimal guards, we should be safer there than that town centre."

"I'd try to find us some coin tonight," Anise said, "But my dress is back at the clutch warehouse. I don't have my drug supplies."

"Are those difficult to replace?" Garrett asked.

Anise shrugged. "If you know where to go and who to talk to it isn't difficult, for a price." She kept looking out the window. "My concern is that if you're buying all the components at once the apothecaries get suspicious."

Garrett gave her a puzzled look.

"Apothecaries know what their wares are used for," Anise explained. "One or two items alone could have any number of medicinal uses. The entire list for my concoction bought all at once would give them the impression I was doing some nasty acts."

"Isn't your drug like a sleeping draught?" Garrett asked.

"Not exactly," Anise replied with a sinister smile on her face. "It's a mixture of aphrodisiacs, opioids, painkillers, and components to induce prolonged sleep."

Garrett nodded. His eyes were glazed. "I'm starting to feel some fatigue."

"Fatigue," Anise scoffed. "You look ready to sleep for a week."

The fire crackled in the hearth. Garrett added a handful of wood. In a moment the fire swelled and the heat radiated several feet into the room. Anise checked to ensure the windows were closed. They spread one blanket out on the floor, huddled together, draped the second blanket over them, and tried to sleep.

Anise sprang up. She sat staring at the window. "Did you see that?"

"See what?" Garrett mumbled.

"I thought I saw a light?"

"Of course you see light, there's a fire burning."

"I meant something shimmering," Anise said.

"Most likely a shadow or reflection from the flames changing as they burn," Garrett said. "As we said, sleep tonight. Tomorrow we worry about money and food."

Garrett's eyes closed. He snored loudly. Anise lay beside him, sharing the blanket and warmth, but not his ease in attaining rest.

Chapter 12 – Exile

Anise tossed and turned most of the night; Garrett managed to sleep soundly. When morning came, Garrett opened his eyes to see Anise sitting up adding sticks to the fire. "Were you cold?" he asked.

"No," Anise replied. "I just didn't sleep well. Those flickering reflections from the fire on the windows kept tricking me into thinking there was a light outside. This isn't a safe area of town."

"You can try to get some rest now," Garrett offered. "I'll stand watch. We can take turns tonight."

"Let's get the bed frame to town," Anise replied. "Exhausted as I am, my stomach is rumbling and the hunger would keep me awake."

Garrett moved the headboard away from the wall. He grabbed both the head and foot boards at one end with the wood behind him. "I'll take the front end, you get the rear."

Anise picked up the other ends. She stood between the pieces facing Garrett. They rustled and adjusted their grips.

"Ready?" Garrett asked.

"Lead the way," Anise said.

A few blocks toward town they saw people walking in and out of an old warehouse. They neared the warehouse and heard a voice behind them. "That's a nice piece for the exchange."

After a brief silence, Garrett replied with a simple, "thank you."

"What're you hoping to get for that?" the voice asked.

"Depends on who's asking," Anise replied. "You thinking of making us an offer?"

Garrett set the bed ends down and turned around. Anise kept the pieces steady and turned her head. The man who approached them wore a knee-length overcoat. He had a scar on his chin and a patch over his left eye.

"I watch the exchange," he said. "Sometimes I see wares of interest."

"Does this interest you?" Anise prodded.

The man stroked his chin. His right hand stroked his left arm up and down. His eyes darted back and forth. His face scrunched in all different directions.

"Are you unwell?" Garrett asked.

"Pondering the price I could get for this," he replied.

"Price you could get?" Garrett questioned.

"I have a cart," the man began. "Items of interest to me are ones that will fetch more coin in town than this exchange house. I may be able to offer you more than they do, I just need to consider resale value, transportation cost, and of course a little something for me."

"So, you suppose you could haul this to town and get a better price than here?" Anise asked.

"Who in the Old Quarter will pay much for this?" the man asked. "In town, there are merchants, craftsmen, traders, soldiers of rank, factory owners, all manner of people with affluence and coin. Once, those people lived here too; those days are long past."

Garrett scratched his chin. "What are you prepared to offer?"

"Three tin chits," the man answered quickly.

"Think you could manage a fourth?" Anise asked with a kind smile. "We'd have liked a whole bronze Guinea."

The man's mouth and eyes scrunched briefly. "Alright," he said with a nod. "Four tin chits, I'll even give it to you as two chits and ten copper pennies so you're able to haggle. You need to load those onto my cart."

Anise and Garrett exchanged a quick glance and nod. "Agreed," Garrett said as he extended his hand to shake.

The man shook his hand. Garrett and Anise picked up the bed frame pieces. The man walked over to a nearby horse-drawn cart and pointed without saying a word. Anise and Garrett rested the footboard against the cart's wheel. They loaded the headboard first and then put the footboard in. They walked to the man. His hand was in a coin purse.

He handed Garrett a handful of loose coins. "As we agreed." The man mounted the cart and prepared to depart.

Garrett looked down at his hand. He fished through the coins with his finger. "Hey, there's only two chits and eight pennies here. It was supposed to be ten."

"Walk away," the man threatened, reaching for a large club. "Two pennies aren't worth the trouble." As he spoke two other men walked up to the cart.

"Problem, boss?" one of them asked.

"Three against two," Garrett whispered to Anise.

"No drugs, no auras, no powers," Anise whispered back.

Garrett took a step back. He bit his lower lip and scowled at the man on the wagon. "You're right. Two pennies isn't enough for me to waste my time teaching you a lesson." He turned to Anise. "Let's get on with our day."

Garrett patted down his clothing; he had no pockets and no purse. The coins jingled in his hand. He cocked his head slightly toward Anise. "I don't suppose you have pockets."

Anise patted herself down. "I got this outfit from the clutch. I'll have to check." She patted and squeezed at her blouse and pants. "Found one," she said patting her right hip.

Garrett handed Anise the pile of coins. She shoved them in her pocket as they walked into the exchange building.

"What is this?" Garrett asked.

"A market," Anise replied.

"I've never seen a market like this before."

Anise sighed, her head slowly turning to survey the crowd. "It's a market for those who can't make it to a real market. There should be some amount of crop food dropped off by the farmers on their way to town. The rest will be items people have sold to have coin for survival."

"We should see what we can find," Garrett said. "Eighteen pennies worth of coin doesn't spread very far."

"We have a choice to make," Anise said. "We can see what supplies for my drug we can find, or we can buy some food supplies and try begging for scraps."

Garrett's teeth clenched inside his closed mouth. His skin wrinkled around his cheekbones and eyes. "Not much of a choice. I could manage bodyguard work, but I can't be found by the garrison."

Anise nodded. "Alright, we should see what supplies we can manage with this."

They walked into the exchange building. It was a vast indoor market. Tables and stalls of all kinds were erected in blocks of rows and columns. No signage existed to provide direction, and there was no visible organizational pattern. Fruit and meat vendors were spread about. There were merchants with knives and other tools visible but again dispersed among the crowd of stalls.

"How are we to find anything?" Garrett muttered.

"This gives us an advantage," Anise said.

Garrett looked at her with a puzzled expression.

"If there are several merchants here with apothecary supplies, I may be able to find what we need without alarming any of them."

Garrett smiled and gestured toward the market with his arm. "Lead the way."

Anise surveyed the nearest row of stalls. Garrett followed. They wandered through the sea of people assessing the products on the tables. Anise focused primarily on the tables and wares for sale. Garrett kept his eyes up, alert, visually scrutinizing each member of the crowd.

"What are you doing?" Anise hissed.

"Watching for thieves and pickpockets," Garrett replied. "Many people here are in dire straits, others are likely here to take advantage of them."

"You look like a guard," she scolded. "That face, that posture. You look like you're infiltrating this place. Stop before you scare the vendors. I can't negotiate with them if they're unnerved and over cautious."

"Wouldn't they assume I'm your bodyguard?" Garrett asked.

"If I can afford a bodyguard I can afford their price," Anise growled under her breath. "It stifles my ability to negotiate. You look more official than intimidating. More like a soldier than a mercenary."

Garrett's voice got louder. "Well, I was..."

"Stop," Anise gasped. She immediately put her hand on the nearest item on a table. "We need to see this cloth!"

Garrett stood stunned as Anise checked over several samples of cloth on a vendor's table. She held some up against herself and looked down.

The vendor approached from behind his table. "How much would the fine lady like?"

"Um," Anise stopped and put the cloth down. "It's beautiful, it really is. I just don't think we can afford it today. I'll be looking for you when I can buy material for a new dress."

Anise walked away with a sad expression. Garrett followed. They walked through a few rows of tables, out to the perimeter of the room.

"You need to be more careful," Anise warned. "People in a place like this don't want to hear the word soldier."

"I'm sorry," Garrett muttered. "I grew up an orphan, but these markets were not places I frequented."

"Fortunately, I have," Anise said. "Drugs are much harder to find in a legitimate marketplace."

"If I'm not your bodyguard this time, what role am I to act out?" Garrett asked.

"My husband," Anise said with a smirk. "Look defeated and miserable. When you observe the crowd look more worried, almost afraid. That's the way to blend with this lot."

Garrett nodded. "Should we pretend to be talking? Pretend we are trying to budget our coins? Maybe even go back and ask that cloth vendor's price?"

"Now, that isn't a bad plan," Anise said. "First let's look like we're talking about shopping." She pointed to the cloth vendor. "We need to make anyone suspicious of us think we're part of this crowd."

Garrett pointed in the direction of a bakery table they had passed. "Like this? Provide the impression you're pondering cloth and I'm more interested in bread?"

Anise nodded, then frowned. "I'll try to appear sad about the cloth. This standing at the wall needs to stop soon. I think anyone observing us should be fairly convinced."

"Hopefully their attention is focused elsewhere when you meet with any apothecaries," Garrett said. He pointed in the direction of a few produce stands.

They walked back into the sea of people, tables, and stalls. Anise went straight to the cloth vendor and examined the piece she held earlier. She spoke with a tremor in her voice. "H...how much?"

The vendor's eyes rolled slightly. "Two chits for the bolt."

"We can't afford that," Garrett said sternly. He put his hand on Anise's shoulder. "I'm sorry, darling, but we just don't have enough for that. Maybe some other time, after I've found work."

"Do you have a price you could pay?" the vendor asked. "It won't be this material, but I do have more modestly priced options."

Anise and Garrett looked at each other. "Three pennies at the highest," Anise said.

The vendor stroked his chin while turning and looking at his wares. He ran his hands through a few bolts of cloth. "Nothing nice for that sum. You'll have to save up. Sorry, I can't help you."

Anise nodded slightly. Her cheeks puffed and she exhaled. With a disheartened look on her face, she led Garrett away.

Several tables down they found an old lady selling what she called *love tonics*. Anise approached, slowly creping her hand over the vials and bottles on the table. She handled one, then another looking for absent labels. "What are these? Some sensual perfume?"

"No, Child," the old lady said with a cackle. "These are tonics. You have a man drink them, and he loses control of his faculties and inhibitions." She glanced at Garrett then back to Anise. "They make for very enjoyable nights, Deary." She winked and let out another short cackle.

Anise raised her eyebrows with intrigue. "How much?"

"For you, child," the lady said as she pushed a small vial into Anise's hand, "the first sample is free. There should be two doses worth in there. Come see me when you need more."

Anise smiled. "Thank you. I'm sure we'll meet again."

As they walked away Garrett nudged Anise. "That seemed successful."

Anise nodded. "As part of my drug, this should last four or five doses. Very successful."

"We need to stop for some food as well as the other medicines," Garrett commented. "We don't have the pans to bake bread, we will need some."

Anise glared at him. "My stomach is growling at me too. We will handle food and drug shopping the best we can."

"Eighteen pennies," Garrett sighed. "Going to be hard to stretch that."

"I've stretched less," Anise said. "Surely we both have."

Garrett plodded forward silently. There was a constant droning noise within the exchange building. The sounds of multiple transactions blended into one constant source of indiscernible noise. They came across a produce table.

"Vegetables?" the man asked as they walked by.

Anise surveyed the table. "They look old. How long since they were harvested?"

"Long, but not too long," the man replied. "Today's their last day. I can give you a good price."

Garrett sifted his hand through the vegetables on the table. "We can take some of the carrots and potatoes," he said. "Maybe a few onions too."

"That and I'll add a few ears of corn and a couple turnips for two pennies," the man offered eagerly.

Anise fished two copper pennies from her pocket and handed them to the farmer. "Agreed."

The farmer placed the vegetables in a small sack and handed it to Anise. She and Garrett continued walking through the market stalls.

They came across another apothecary stand. Anise leaned toward the elderly man standing behind the table. "I'm looking for opium," she whispered. "Do you know where I can find any?"

The old man's eyes narrowed. He shifted his gaze from Anise to Garrett. "You've come to the wrong place, Missy. Take that poorly disguised guard and be on your way." He waved his hand as he backed away.

"He's not a guard," Anise hissed, maintaining a quiet voice. "Do you have what I'm asking for?"

The man paused. "I want nothing to do with a guard or your attempt at entrapment. Leave me alone."

Garrett stepped forward. "I'm not a guard, but I could find one if there's going to be a problem."

"Threats don't work on me, young man."

"Please, sir," Anise begged. "Do you have what I need? I don't need much."

The man eyed them both. He sighed. "What quantity?" he eventually mumbled.

"Two, maybe three small doses," Anise replied. "Enough for some fun, but not a large amount."

"Later today there should be a man around behind the building. He prefers to avoid those who are shopping for basic supplies to maintain some anonymity."

Anise nodded and walked away.

"Thank you," Garrett whispered, passing the old man and keeping pace with Anise.

"Bread, and a sleeping aid," Anise whispered to Garrett. "We should find the bread first. I don't want to be seen going from one apothecary to another; looks suspicious."

Garrett followed silently. They walked through the rows of tables and salespeople. The exchange became busier as the day progressed. A lot of women in tattered dresses went through; most could be heard pleading for price reductions. Some of the women had children with them, most ranging from about six to twelve years old. The children asked for work in exchange for pennies or products. Some of the vendors dismissed the requests, while others sat and allowed the children to organize their wares, sweep scraps from their table area, or unload more products from carts outside. One lady with vials of various tonics had a young girl, maybe seven years old, wiping the vials with a rag to make them more appealing. One baker employed a boy of about ten years to stage the loaves of bread and other items making the table look its best.

"I was one of these children," Anise sighed. "It seems like a lifetime ago. Find a generous baker or farmer, keep their table its best, treat their customers well, and have fresh bread or a penny for my time."

Garrett took in his surroundings. "The orphanage I grew up in didn't allow us to go too far from the building. Boys like John and I begged for scraps. Some boys resorted to pickpocketing, but those who were caught took some serious beatings."

"It was nice on cold or rainy days," Anise said, starting to reminisce. "To be warm and dry. I was never sure about my bed, but when I was here, I knew something would go in my belly."

As they spoke, they walked up to the baker's table with the boy arranging the bread.

"Good day, sir, ma'am," the boy said with a cheerful smile. "Can I help you today?" The baker stood by but observed the boy.

"We would like some bread," Anise said, pointing to the far end of the table. "I would like the two loaves at the end."

The boy looked at the baker, he mouthed the word three without a sound. The boy looked at Anise. "Three copper pennies, please."

Anise fished the coins from her pocket and handed them to the boy. Garrett held up the bag with the vegetables. The boy took the coins and loaded the bread into the bag. "Come back again," the boy said as he handed the coins to the baker.

Garrett nodded at the boy and the baker as he started walking.

"Thank you," Anise said, walking away.

"Have a wonderful day," the boy called.

They walked to a corner and turned. "I still need sleeping aids and maybe some painkillers for my drug," Anise mumbled.

"And the opium salesman out back," Garrett muttered. "We have enough food for today and tomorrow. Two chits and three pennies left. Just need to be careful about spending.

They came across another table with small flasks and vials. Anise watched the man behind the table polishing some empty vials. "Excuse me, sir," Anise said, feigning innocence. "I'm having trouble sleeping lately, would you have anything to help me sleep?"

The man finished wiping the flask in his hand and set it down. "May I ask why aren't you sleeping? Worried about what's outside creeping?" He smirked at his own joke.

Anise stared surprised. "I don't know. Worry about the way this town is I suppose. Concern for where my next meal will come from, whether I have sufficient firewood or not, when my husband will find work again..." she paused and glanced at Garrett, he took the queue, his eyes flashed, and Anise recoiled. "The concerns of an ever difficult life."

"I have something, one drop is all you need. It's distilled ten times for potency and speed."

"What size vial? How much?" Anise yawned. She wiped her puffy eyes dry. "I haven't slept well for some time."

"I have a vial with a dropper in the stopper," the man rhymed. "Four or five doses, that is it. All it costs is one tin chit."

"You like to rhyme, don't you?" Garrett asked.

"In a world of woe, let it lighten your heart. The rhyming apothecary, call me, Bart." He giggled at the end.

"We'll call you if it works...and if it doesn't," Garrett said with a glint in his eye. He quickly turned and started away, Anise paid Bart and scurried to catch Garrett.

"Outside?" Anise huffed as she caught up.

"One chit, two pennies," Garrett commented. "Opium price, then see about any other food."

"Maybe bowls and spoons too," Anise said.

Garrett nodded his head in agreement. They walked out of the exchange building and around back. Behind the building, there were wagon loading areas.

Anise pointed as they drew near the cart area. "Beyond those carts, I see some secluded areas, presumably for garbage when the warehouse was operational. That may be where our man is." She quickened her pace to almost a jog. Garrett walked at his regular pace behind her.

Anise stopped in front of a man with a black, knee-length coat. "What wares do you sell?"

"I deal in items one typically doesn't ask about so bluntly, young lady," he replied evasively.

Garrett reached Anise. "Is this our vendor?"

"You look like a guard," the man observed, waving his hand around. "That posture, that stare, even your question, they all stink of soldier training."

"I'm nothing," Garrett said. "My father was a guard. I always looked up to him. My mannerisms are learned behaviour from him, may he rest in peace." Garrett tried to force a tear, but his eyes could barely water. He gulped and wiped his eye dry.

Anise took his hand. "It's alright, darling. Don't dwell on this dark day. He wouldn't want you to be like this." She turned to the man in the coat. "Today's the anniversary of his father's death. It happened right in front of him. He was very young. We just want something to ease the painful memories. You looked like you might be able to help."

The man scratched his chin. "I may be able to satisfy your needs. I assume you have very little coin and you're looking for some degree of generosity on my part?"

"We aren't rich," Anise replied. "Any generosity you can show would be greatly appreciated. We're hoping to be in a position to repay the kindnesses we've been shown in the near future."

The man slipped a small paper-wrapped package into Anise's hand. "First taste is on the house."

Garrett nodded. Anise said, "thank you." They walked away.

Garrett's stomach growled. He cupped his arm around it. "Bowls and spoons, maybe meat, we can make a soup or stew. At least we'll eat."

Anise's mouth watered. "Just the words are making my hunger worse. Want a bite of bread before we go back in?"

They took some bread from the bag and broke pieces off. The instant they swallowed their hands grabbed their stomachs and their faces twisted.

"We haven't eaten in so long," Anise groaned. "Our bodies will need to be gently reintroduced to food."

They put the bread in the bag and walked back into the exchange. Two tables in, there was someone with kitchen goods. Bowls, spoons, a ladle, knives. Garrett walked over quickly.

"How much?" he asked.

"How much for what?" the lady behind the table asked.

"A ladle, two bowls and spoons, a cutting knife," Garrett replied.

The lady giggled. "Starter package, Congratulations you two."

Anise squinted for a second, then wrapped her arms around Garrett's arm. "Thank you," she said. "How much for the starter package?"

"You're such a lovely couple," the lady said. "You look too sweet to be in a decrepit place like this..." she paused as her tone turned to disgust. She took a breath. "Pardon me, I've just seen a lot of lives ruined lately. It's refreshing to see new life and happy faces. Normally I sell the lot for seven pennies, but I can sell for six."

Anise and Garrett exchanged glances. Anise handed the lady the remaining chit and one of the two pennies she had. "Thank you," she said as they made the transaction.

Anise and Garrett left the exchange. Garrett tilted his head. "We seem to have just managed. Let's get fed and warm that house. We can worry about more coin tomorrow."

They walked back to the house in silence. Anise prepared the vegetables while Garrett fetched water from the well down the street. Garrett prepared the fire and Anise added everything but the bread to the pot. Anise slowly stirred the would-be soup while Garrett went out and fetched sticks and pieces of old crates for the fire.

When the vegetables were boiled into something resembling a soup they took a bowl, a spoon, and some bread. They sat by the hearth and ate.

The sun slowly set while Anise and Garrett huddled together and fell asleep.

Chapter 13 - Cruelty

The sun shone through the window into Anise's eyes. She blinked as she moved out of the light's path. Garrett was gone. Anise jumped up to search for him. There was fresh wood in the hearth fire and a kettle boiling. "He found a kettle," she mumbled, wiping the sleep from her eyes. "I wonder what he's boiling water for."

The door opened. Anise spun to see Garrett walking in with a load of old boards from broken crates. He smiled at her. "Good morning." Garrett walked across the room and dropped the wood on the floor. "We'll be warm tonight," he commented.

Anise wiped her eyes. "What's the hot water for?"

"Thought it might be nice to wash up with," Garrett replied. "If you're going to revert to your seduce and rob routine it would serve your interests to be presentable."

Anise's face scrunched. She glared at Garrett for a moment, then laughed. "Something else we didn't worry about as Infernals. How should we spend the day?"

"You can rest if you need to," Garrett replied. "I intend to go the short distance to the forest and see what I can find."

"Hunting?" Anise whispered. "What if you're caught?"

"Penalty for poaching is the same as being caught as a deserter. They can only kill me once."

Anise stared blankly. "I suppose so." She poured some hot water into her bowl and grabbed a rag. "My intent was to find suitable grounds for my own hunt."

"What are you planning?" Garrett asked.

"Find some old contacts," Anise replied. "I want to know what territory is safe to work and what areas will be problematic."

"Problematic?" Garrett repeated.

"Some streetwalkers are territorial, hire muscle, they aren't welcoming, to say the least."

Garrett's eyes widened, he nodded and sighed. "Sounds as though there are many unspoken rules to consider."

Anise gave a little smile, wiped her face and arms, and left the house. She walked through the streets, occasionally reaching into her pocket and handling the lone copper penny from the bed sale. Each caress of it brought a smile to her face, which she quickly dismissed, releasing the coin.

She approached a building with two women standing out front. Both wore flashy dresses. Anise approached and saw their faces. "Cassandra? Victoria?"

One turned and made eye contact with Anise. "That's Classy and Vixen, to you," she said with a smile.

Anise chuckled. "Still using the pet names I see."

"The men have come to expect them. We get more generous customers this way," said Classy. Her dress was a pink colour, covering most of her body. Her blonde hair flowed halfway down her back.

Vixen took a step toward Anise. Her emerald-coloured dress flowed as she walked. She tucked a strand of her brown hair behind her ear. "We feared you were dead."

"I've been through quite the experience," Anise sighed. "Something I'd rather not discuss if that's alright with you."

Both ladies looked at her stunned. "Your drug didn't work this time?" Vixen asked. "Were you injured?"

"It wasn't the drug," Anise replied. She stared skyward for a moment, then at her feet, surprised by the emotions she felt. "I thought I found a place to belong. In the end, though, I'm on the streets and penniless again."

Classy walked over and hugged Anise. "You poor dear. Is there any way we can help?"

"Where would it be safe for me to work tonight?" Anise asked. "I've managed enough supplies to get back on my feet..." she said with a smile, "or on some part of me."

Vixen stifled a laugh. "Drug's effects difficult to time?"

"Different people react differently. Stall tactics only last so long," Anise replied. "I shouldn't stay long. I still have preparations to make."

"About three blocks away from the tavern we used to work near there's an old grain warehouse," Classy said, pointing down the road. "Farmers aren't using it anymore. It's turned into a gathering place for factory workers looking for a girl. They get paid well too."

Anise's head perked up. There was a gleam in her eyes. "How well?"

"There's a lot of factories paying almost slave wages, two and a half copper a day; you'd do better on a farm, two pennies three meals and a bed. Others are paying well, men work six days and they have a bronze guinea," Classy said.

"How do you earn half a penny?" Anise asked.

"Paid by the week," replied Vixen. "We get one or two good working days now. Then they're all out of coin until next payday."

Anise smirked. "Nine pennies at those low-wage factories doesn't leave much to spend on quality goods like you two."

"I've had to lower my price," Vixen pouted. "At least they're usually so tired from the long hours, they don't last. Can service two or three a night, if they don't pass out first. They pass out, you move on which balances my purse weight."

Anise laughed. "I'll keep that in mind, especially if they're carrying guineas."

"Some tea?" Cassandra asked, motioning toward the building.

"No, thank you. I need to prepare."

Anise walked away. Judging from the sun it was close to midday, maybe shortly after. She walked briskly through the streets and back to the abandoned house.

The house was empty, chilled by a cool draft. There was still a glow from the embers in the hearth. Anise gathered some of the sticks in the room and placed a few around the glowing coals. She dropped to her knees and blew. The coals radiated heat and red light. She blew again, and again. A small flame emerged and soon flame crackled from a stick. Anise prepared the fire and reheated the soup in the pot.

When the soup was warm, Anise had another bowl along with some leftover bread. She sat and watched the fire crackle. The spoon sank into the soup. Anise sat motionless, mesmerized by the flames.

As Garrett dropped an armload of branches, Anise jumped. She spilled cold soup on her lap.

"Sorry I startled you," Garrett said.

"What time is it?" Anise asked.

"Nearly sundown," Garrett replied with a puzzled look. "I managed to spear us a few rabbits," he said holding up four rabbits by their ears.

"Use two sell two?" Anise asked. "Even though there's not much meat the pelts have value."

Garrett looked at the hearth; the fire was down to a few flickers among the glowing embers and coals. "Did I wake you?" he asked placing a few sticks in the fire.

"I'm not sure I was asleep," Anise said. "I was staring at the fire, and then everything went blank."

"Sounds like sleep," Garrett said. "You were tired, we both are."

"Almost sundown and I don't have my drug made!" Anise gasped. "I don't have time now. How could I let this happen?"

"Don't go tonight," Garrett suggested.

"We need the coin," Anise protested. "We need to be able to live."

"It's dangerous," Garrett said. "I don't like the thought of you being hurt."

Anise's eyes widened. Stunned for a moment, she replied. "We fought Shamblers, we fought Shifters, we spent the night in a den of succubi, and you're concerned about me being injured doing this?"

"Were you injured before?" Garrett asked. "Without the drug, what would you do?"

"I've been hurt before," Anise admitted. "The drug didn't work very quickly. The man was drunk and forceful. I tried to stall. He pressed me and tore my dress. He did all the things I hated about this life. All the things which drove me to serve them what they deserved."

"Only once?" Garrett asked, placing a couple more branches in the fireplace.

"More than once," Anise admitted. "There have been several occasions. I had some mishaps early on. The drug in the wrong drink, mix ratios were off, the man didn't want to drink so he could get the full experience he paid for..." she trailed off.

As Anise trailed off Garrett blinked and pursed his lips. "Hearing that I'm relieved you're not going out tonight. I don't like seeing you hurt."

"Those foul excuses for men deserve what they get," Anise snapped. "A few bruises is a small price to pay for justice being served."

"Justice, or vengeance?" Garrett asked. "Were you being an avenger for justice by choice, or was your demon blood influencing your behaviour?"

Anise blinked, her eyes widened, and her mouth gaped open. After a moment of silence, she blinked again. "Now that I'm aware of my heritage, I imagine there was some element of sadism incorporated into my motivation. I always thought it was a way to make a living and to punish."

"From our altercation with those men a while back, I assume you made some enemies," Garrett commented.

"Would you appreciate waking in an alley penniless?" Anise asked. "They're just lucky I only debated castration instead of practicing it." Her eyes glinted and she let out a mischievous grin.

Garrett's head pulled back and his eyes bugged. "I've never seen you act or speak so menacingly."

"I required many different appearances, shall we say," Anise replied. She walked over and stroked Garrett's cheek with her finger. She brushed the side of his body with hers. "I had to be the sweet, sensual, playful little woman," she whispered. She then stepped back, quickly drawing her dagger. With the dagger only inches away from Garrett's groin she continued. "I also had to stop any nonsense before the situation escalated too far," she growled.

Garrett took two steps back. "I can see you honed your control over your attitude very well. Tonight we can try to rest. The soup is still warm and we can add some rabbit meat. We will get some money for the others and pelts tomorrow. You don't need to return to that sordid situation."

"You sound like you care," Anise said.

Garrett walked to the hearth and quietly tended the fire for a moment. "We don't know how long we'll be without our abilities. This expulsion could be temporary or permanent. Until we know, and especially if we're stuck like this, you're the person I trust the most. I won't let anything avoidable happen."

"You won't let anything happen?" Anise questioned. "Are you trying to forbid me from going out?"

"I didn't use the word forbid," Garrett pointed out.

"We need money to survive," Anise argued. "Dangerous as it may be, this is the fastest way to get a good haul of coin."

"I can hunt," Garrett offered, holding up the rabbits.

"Will you be successful daily?" Anise snapped. "Or will we go from feasting to starving? There's barely any meat on those things anyway."

"At least there's less risk," Garrett grumbled.

"Less risk?" Anise scoffed. "You're poaching. If you're caught you'll be executed publicly. If anyone recognized you as a deserter the method of execution would become much more severe than a simple hanging. You'd be tortured to death on display to keep order."

"That's my risk to take," Garrett snapped.

"And walking the streets is my risk to take." Anise countered. Her eyes fluttered. Tears began running down her face. "What would I have if... if anything happened to you?"

Garrett stood stunned for a second. He walked over and began wiping the tears from Anise's face. Garrett wrapped his arms around her quivering body. "It seems we both know there needs to be risk. Neither of us wants the other placed in danger. What other alternatives can we explore?"

"I refuse to beg," Anise said. "If avoidable I would rather not sell my hair either."

"Labourer jobs are usually available," Garrett suggested. "But one day's rabbit pelts might equal a week's hard labour in coin."

Garrett motioned for Anise to sit. He sat beside her, took out a knife and skinned the first rabbit as he spoke. "How much might a single pelt sell for?"

"You'll need a few for something like a stoll," Anise commented. "The exchange may have traders, but not a furrier. Poor people don't have money for furs. They won't sell frequently either. Furs are seldom bought, not an everyday staple."

"Belittle the idea if you must," Garrett said as he carefully peeled the rabbit's pelt from the meat, "it's an idea that doesn't involve prostitution."

Anise shoved Garrett away as she sprang to her feet. "I never was, nor will I ever be a prostitute!"

"You met men, you spent time with them for money, what else would you call it?"

"I managed to avoid being bedded," Anise replied, "most of the time."

"What would you have called yourself?" Garrett asked.

"A seductress and a thief," Anise answered. "What about you? Before being a soldier what were you?"

"I was back and forth between beggar and thief," Garrett said. "Some days I managed an honest day's labour, but it was rare. I'd seen John, and what happened to him in a factory; I was scared to work there. Other children too; they get the dangerous work in the gears of the machines because of their tiny hands."

"This world has become so dangerous," Anise observed. "Before the factories, before these large towns, people farmed. Machines, grinding gears, mangled children, that black smoke that fills the air...they call it progress, but what's progressing?"

Garrett stopped skinning the rabbit. He stared into the crackling fire. "I don't have the answer."

"The cruelty of this new world is breaking the common folk," Anise said. "Cities and large towns came with factories. Homes abandoned, workers maimed and killed by machinery, and smoke that causes sickness. People flock to the city to have a better life, and they can barely find a suitable place to sleep."

"I heard you," Garrett replied.

"I hate these sights," Anise grumbled.

"Life on a farm would be simpler," Garrett offered. "But with new machines, there's less demand for hands."

"Tonight I suppose you finish skinning those, I'll prepare my drug, we get some sleep, and we try the exchange building in the morning," Anise said.

"I don't like the drug idea," Garrett said shaking his head. "We did spend the money on ingredients though. We did commit to at least one batch. I hope it works and you're careful."

"I was always careful," Anise replied. "You know it is possible to fail even if you've done everything the proper way."

"How often would you fail?" Garrett asked.

Anise's chest heaved as she took a deep breath. She blinked. "Too often for my liking."

"Then you shouldn't go back to that life," Garrett insisted. He looked to the hearth and threw another stick in. He watched as the stick ignited and the fire crackled. "At least, not permanently."

"How else are we supposed to survive?" Anise asked. "We can't sell our weapons, and we have nothing else of value. Our human lives ended as soon as we were brought to the clutch."

"We could go on the road, to a new town," Garrett offered.

"To do what?" Anise asked. "I'm not going to work in some factory, and I don't think you want to slave away in one either."

Garrett continued skinning the rabbits. His face scrunched. "I could take a job as a soldier."

"We would have to go weeks away for you to avoid recognition and desertion penalties," Anise said. "We won't survive that long on the road with no food or coin."

Garrett set down the rabbit and knife. He stood up and paced around the room. "We need a plan, a feasible solution to this. What options are realistic and available?"

"Poverty or thievery," Anise replied, hanging her head. "My only skill is using my body and drugs to separate men from their money. You're a warrior, a soldier, but you're branded a deserter and wanted. Options don't exist, solutions require options."

"Highwayman or sellsword," Garrett muttered. "Neither sounds overly pleasant."

Anise started mixing her ingredients. "Our best option is for me to find a wealthy target."

Garrett gritted his teeth behind his scrunched lips. He didn't speak another word. He continued to work on the rabbits until all four were skinned.

The pot on the fire created an aroma which drew Anise and Garrett's attention back to their hunger. They filled bowls and ate the concoction in the pot.

The meal and evening held little conversation. Each time they met eyes they looked away. Garrett added more wood to the fire. The crackling blaze kept the room warm. The uneasy silence lasted until they prepared for bed.

As Anise lay down she stared toward the window intently.

"What're you staring at?" Garrett asked.

Anise squinted and maneuvered her head. "I keep seeing an odd flickering light. I wonder if it's simply the lamps reflecting in the glass, or if someone is out there with a torch, or if something else is transpiring."

Garrett craned his neck and stared at the window. "It's a flickering light. Flame of some sort. It looks too small for a torch, so I'd wager the street lamp flickering is causing it." He laid back down and pulled the tattered blanket over his face.

Anise sat watching the flickering light from the window. Mesmerized, she sat until she fell asleep and crumpled into a ball on the floor.

Chapter 14 - Light

lickers of light glimmering and dancing through the windows kept Anise awake much of the night. She mumbled her thoughts as she wrestled to calm her mind. "Streetwalker life? Make a new life? Can this be a viable solution? Is there another alternative?"

Garrett stirred but didn't respond.

Anise looked out the window. "Lights in the night, what should I do? What will make my life bearable? What must I do to avoid returning to the gutter?"

The lights continued to captivate Anise as she gave up trying to sleep and paced. The fire was low, she placed more branches and a broken board into the hearth. The wood crackled as it ignited, spreading warmth throughout the room.

Anise rubbed her hands together and held them to the fire. She looked at the small amount of wood left; it wouldn't last another night. She peered at her bag and the mixed ingredients. "Sometimes the risk is necessary," she muttered to herself snatching up the concoction.

She crept out the door and trotted down the streets. There were other streetwalkers out on various corners but few men wandering the area. The flames in the street lamps combined well with the shining stars in the sky. It was a clear night sky. Anise looked up and stopped walking. "Maybe life outside of town would be nicer, more beautiful."

"Excuse me," a voice said from behind her.

Anise turned to see a man behind her. His clothes were dirty and had several small tears. "Yes, sir?"

"Are you *working*?" he asked

"Define *working*. I'm clearly not here to light the lamps; no torch or stick."

"I've got a stick you can work with," the man said, gesturing toward his groin.

Anise grimaced at the gesture, then faked a smile. She purposefully shifted her gaze down then up to meet his leering eyes. "Those sticks require more coin than the ones lighting the streets."

The man chuckled. He pulled a small pouch from inside his coat. He jingled the pouch in his hand. The telltale clinking sound as the pouch shook caused Anise's face to perk up. "Tin?"

"I've got the tin, and even the bronze if you're worthy," he snickered.

"I can be worth a grinny," Anise said with a smile. "We should get a drink. What's a night of fun without a few drinks?"

"I don't want a drink," the man protested. "I want to be fully aware and in control. I want to enjoy what I'm paying for."

"Aren't you paying for a fun evening?" Anise asked.

"I'm paying to bed a whore," the man replied. "I don't need a drink, I don't need talk, I just need a place to lay you down." He jingled the sack, several coins could be heard.

"Noise from that pouch is enticing," Anise commented. "How do I know there's tin or bronze? Could be a sack of pennies."

The man's expression changed. He no longer eyed Anise with a lustful smile, his eyes widened, his teeth gritted. "Don't question me, whore." He lunged forward and used his free hand to grab Anise's throat. He buried his other hand in her stomach while slamming her against a nearby wall.

Anise gasped. "Why?"

"Whores don't speak," he replied, slapping her across the face with the hand holding the coin purse. He kept his hand at her throat and started opening his pants. Anise scratched and clawed at the hand and wrist, but the man held his grip firmly.

Struggling to breathe, Anise tried to scramble back. but The wall behind and the man's grip pinned her in place. Her eyes fluttered and became heavy.

He threw her to the ground. "I want you to feel this. I'm not letting you pass out."

He knelt down at her feet and pushed her dress up. As the dress moved higher and the man inched closer Anise thrust both legs into his chest. He fell back on his seat. He grunted on impact then returned Anise's kick. She let out a small squeal and both arms wrapped around her stomach. She rolled to one side and started to crawl away.

Jumping on top of Anise, he spun her to her back and used both hands to choke her. Flailing her arms and legs Anise struggled and hit the man in various places. His grip tightened and she began to cough and gasp for air. Her arms and legs flailed, but the world edged to black. He pulled her head up and drove it to the ground.

"Make this a little smoother, will you?" he asked. "The more I have to work the less coin I'm going to be leaving you with."

Anise grunted. Her eyelids flickered. She head weaved from side to side. She reached for her dagger; it wasn't there. Her hand motions were frantic.

"That's better," the man commented. "You get that dress up, and the fun can begin."

"Li-li-th," Anise mouthed. "Mah-ther...he-hel-help."

He kissed and licked Anise's cheek and neck. She cringed from the smell of his breath and his rough tongue moving across her neckline. He pawed at her breasts, caressing the dress. His hand crept to her neck and slid down her chest. His fingers wriggled under the fabric of her dress. She shuddered with disgust at his hands exploring her body.

"S-stone," she whispered. "Ch-channel, help, aur-a."

The man ignored her moans. He continued reaching down her dress. Anise tossed and resumed her struggle. The blows to her head and choking left her weakened. She threw her arms about slapping the man; he was unaffected.

"Pay-trun," Anise murmured. "St-one." Her eyes fluttered as she spoke. "Help," she gasped.

"Hold it!" ordered another voice.

The man on Anise spun around to face the voice. His grip loosened and Anise gulped in air. He held her enough to prevent escape. "This has nothing to do with you. This is between the whore and me."

"Unhand that barely conscious woman," the voice replied. A man dressed in an ivory-coloured coat resembling a uniform came from the shadows. He drew a sword and pointed it at Anise's attacker.

The attacker glared at the man and his outfit. "I'm paying for this exchange. That's no soldier's uniform. You some vigilante?"

The man in ivory stood with a stern glare. "I crusade for what is just."

"Well, this is a fair and just business transaction. I'm buying her body for a time. She's being compensated for her troubles."

"Keep your coin and leave...unless you want to lose both your coin and something else you seem to treasure," the man in ivory said changing the aim of the sword from the attacker's throat to his groin.

With air moving in and out of her lungs, Anise's eyes stayed open without fluttering. She assessed the situation.

"Get off of me!" she croaked out. "You're no customer. You're nothing but a savage brute. You don't get your pleasure from my craft, you take it through harm and barbarity."

"You heard the lady," said the man holding the sword. "Leave now, in one piece."

The attacker stayed down on his knees, still between Anise's legs. His eyes narrowed as he too assessed his chances. Alone and with no weapon to defend himself he snarled. "Very well, I'll take my coins and I'll take my leave. Hope the whore plays nicer with you than she did with me."

The attacker slowly rose to his feet and stepped away from Anise. He fastened his pants. The man in ivory maneuvered him away from Anise, sword trained on the attacker.

"Drop the purse," the man with the sword demanded. "The lady was the object of your aggression; she is owed for her suffering."

"I didn't get to finish, she didn't complete the job, she hasn't earned the coin."

The ivory coat shimmered as the man moved. Light from the street lamps reflected on the sword as he flicked his wrist. The blunt edge of the sword snapped against the attacker's hand. He released the purse and grasped his hand as he gasped from the pain. The attacker looked down at his purse on the cobblestone road.

"Leave it," the man in ivory ordered. "Leave it and leave here. I won't tell you again."

Her attacker sized up the man with the sword. Their eyes met and held, a struggle to see who was stronger. Anise rearranged her dress. She leaned against the alley wall. She assessed her injuries while watching the two men face off. She felt around her head and face. Even a gentle touch on her face caused her to wince and hiss from pain.

"Leave!" the man holding the sword barked, pressing then sword into his opponent's chest.

The attacker smirked. "You said you wouldn't tell me again, but you have. You're not going to use that sword. Your intimidation tactic has failed." The attacker took a more relaxed posture and reached for the coin purse he dropped.

Her attacker turned back to Anise shoving her back to the ground even as she fought him. "I don't need an audience," he said tilting his head to look at the man in ivory. Tilting his head, he smirked at the man in ivory until realizing the sword resting on his shoulder. The attacker froze.

The sword slid slowly, along the attacker's cheek. A thin trail of blood crept from the scratch.

"I'll withdraw the sword from your face. You will withdraw from the lady," said the man with the sword. He slowly moved the blade back from the attacker's face, keeping the point aimed directly at him.

The attacker felt his face. Examining the blood on his hand his eyes swelled and his lip quivered. His eyes watered as he cautiously leaned away from the blade. Rising to his feet, he backed away. When he reached the edge of the alley, he ran off into the dark night.

"Everything will be alright, Anise," the man with the sword said.

"How? How do you know my name?" she asked.

"We've been watching you."

"Who are you?" Anise asked as she scrambled to bury the coin purse in her dress.

"Griffith," he replied. "I'm from the flight here in town. I would like you to come with me."

"Flight?" Anise questioned. "What's a flight?"

He ushered her along, looking about and quickening his pace. "A group of Celestials. Everything will be explained once we get back to the cathedral. The streets are not safe."

Anise shook her dress. It flowed and rippled as she straightened out the material. "I'd rather not be going anywhere with anyone unless I have a good reason."

"We need to get you off the streets," Griffith urged. "Where to begin the list? Infernals, Touched, rogue Celestials, mortals like that man I chased off, there are too many ways you could be harmed."

He slowly sheathed his sword and extended an open hand to Anise. "Why would Celestials want to take me in?" Anise asked. "I'm an expelled Infernal. What value do I have for you?"

"That will be explained when we are safely inside the cathedral. I need you to accompany me. I know it sounds peculiar; I'm asking for a little faith."

Anise was a statue. Her eyes locked with Griffith's for a moment. "You know my name, and you know about Infernals and Celestials, but this could be any one of many manners of deception."

"I offer no deception," he affirmed as he sheathed his sword. "I trust the Infernals used your name and personal history to convince you of who they were. I want you to accept me without such tactics."

"Actually," Anise said, "I stabbed one in the shoulder, saw weird oozing liquid where blood should have been, and the demon transformed."

Griffith smiled. "I like your desire to stab demons. That bodes well for the flight."

"I still don't know why you're here," Anise said.

"I want to be able to convince you honestly," Griffith said. "I have no intention of revealing my spirit or wings; you're aware of those and of disguise glyphs Infernals use. There is no proof to be drawn from such an action."

Anise blinked. "The notion of honesty before deception is intriguing, but it would also be an excellent ploy."

"What assurance would be acceptable?" he asked. "How can I show you I mean no ill intent?"

"Manifest your aura," Anise demanded.

"I'm trying to avoid unwanted attention," Griffith stated with a slight snarl.

Anise scowled at him. She crossed her arms. Griffith shook his head slightly and sighed. His eyes closed. A white light emanated from his body, and wings of white feathers sprouted and grew from his shoulders. A yellow ring formed above his head.

"Are you satisfied?" he asked.

"Your sword," Anise insisted as she extended her arm. "Hand it to me."

Griffith slowly drew his sword. He extended the handle to Anise. She wrapped her hand around the hilt and lifted the blade. Anise flicked her wrist and drew the sword back. The blade made a narrow incision along Griffith's palm. He recoiled slightly, then held his hand open exposing a drop of deep red blood. The blood pooled at the tip of the sword and produced a sunlight glow.

"Now are you satisfied?" Griffith asked, suppressing his wings and spirit. The glow stayed around the blood. "That's normal blood with a heavenly spirit cloak emanating from it. That's the farthest substance from oozing demon ichor possible."

Anise handed him the sword. "I'm sorry," she muttered, averting her eyes from his. "I've just seen so many fantastic sights in a short span of time. I don't know what is and isn't real, or even possible, anymore."

Griffith extended his clean arm and put his hand on Anise's shoulder. "There is much to learn about forces beyond that which mortals comprehend. Come, we must get to safety."

Griffith walked briskly out of the alley and down the road. Anise scurried behind him. His stride and pace were longer and faster than she could manage. She lifted her dress and quickened her pace.

Anise followed Griffith down the streets. She slowed and glanced down each alley as they went. At the edge of the Old Quarter, they came upon an abandoned graveyard. There were cobwebs on the trees, shrubs, and headstones. Griffith walked through the open gate and headed toward a decrepit mausoleum.

"Where are you taking me?" Anise whispered.

"This is our flight headquarters," Griffith replied. "Hidden in plain sight, on consecrated ground, where nobody comes or disturbs us."

"Disturbs?" Anise parroted.

"Meaning they won't find us or even stumble upon us by accident," Griffith replied.

He walked up to the mausoleum and pushed the door. The hinges creaked. The door only went part way. Anise noticed the top hinge for the door was broken. Griffith entered, followed by Anise.

Anise's eyes adjusted to the dim room. The door being ajar allowed a shaft of daylight into the mausoleum. The inside was typical for a mausoleum: bones and tattered clothing on shelves, loose bones on the floor, dust collecting on every item and surface, and spiders and other insects crawling about. Some piles of bones were neat, others astray. Dust accumulation varied in depth from shelf to shelf.

"It looks like someone's rummaged through here," Anise observed.

"The appearance that the grave has been robbed deters potential thieves," Griffith replied. "It's a carefully constructed appearance. Any who would ransack this place would assume they're not the first and leave."

"Your system for deterring thieves is an appearance of previous looting?"

"Would you spend time here, rummaging through the bones and tattered clothing of the dead when you believe someone else has already done so?" Griffith stepped up to the table in the middle of the room. He gripped both ends of the table and pushed. It slid back revealing a staircase bathed in white light.

Anise stared in awe, his hand rising to shield her eyes.

"Welcome to the flight," he said, walking down the stairs.

Chapter 15 - Flight

Cautiously, Anise followed Griffith down the stairs. Her hand shielded her eyes from the intense light as she descended.

"How do you even know where the steps are?" she asked. "This light is unimaginable."

"Bathed in the glow, I follow the light. Light is our home, our faith shows us the path," Griffith replied.

"I don't see any path," Anise said as she bobbed her head and squinted around her hand.

"Your conviction is still to be tested," Griffith answered.

Anise stopped. "Conviction? Tested? Why exactly am I here?"

"It is not my place to say," Griffith replied calmly as he stepped through the light. "As I said before, I am asking you for faith."

Anise took two more steps and stopped. She brought her other hand to add cover for her eyes. "The light, the brightness, it's unbearable."

"Faith," Griffith called back.

"Faith in what?" Anise asked raising her voice. "I'm an orphan, I've been beaten down my entire life. Misfortune strikes at every opportunity. How am I to have faith?" She began to sob. "The one place I started to feel belonging just expelled me."

"Have faith in the light," Griffith said. "The light brings salvation from all our troubles."

"How?" Anise questioned. "I don't understand." The sobs muffled her words. "How can I have faith? With everything I've seen and endured, I cannot bring myself to submit in such a manner."

"Close your eyes," Griffith instructed. "Think about good places and times. Think about people you've loved and cherished. The good from your life will guide you. The light inside you will connect with the light in front of you."

Anise closed her eyes. Her eyelids fluttered. She took a step, muttering, "something good, someone good, something about light..."

Griffith stood by, watching her. Anise's steps were slow, asymmetrical, and erratic. Each time a foot went for the floor her leg shook.

"Faith, light, love, faith," Anise murmured as she stumbled through the blinding light. Finally, she stepped through the light into a normally lit room. Griffith stepped in behind her.

"How long is that tunnel?" Anise asked.

"As long as it needs to be," Griffith replied. "When you find your light, you'll be able to enter in a single step."

"How is that possible?" Anise asked.

"I don't understand the divine barrier completely," Griffith replied. "It's a form of limbo, meant to ensure only those of a pure nature may enter."

Anise came to an abrupt halt. "How can I be pure? Lilith, the succubus queen, is my mother. Demon blood courses through my veins. That doesn't seem heavenly or pure to me."

"I can answer that," said a winged man in gold armour as he approached. "My name is Alastair, I am the protector of this flight." Alastair extended his hand to Anise.

Reluctantly, Anise extended her hand and shook hands with Alastair. "Why have I been brought here?"

"Anise Lovejoy, you are not just any Infernal. You have an angelic ancestor in addition to your demonic heritage. You are uniquely capable of attaining the capabilities of both Infernals and Celestials."

Anise's eyes bulged. "I can be both?"

"More correctly, you carry the potential to be either," Alastair replied. "The holy light will only flow through you if you forsake the demonic energy."

"How long have you known about me?" Anise asked. "Did you, like the demons, watch me suffer through all the hardships I've endured? Have you been there, able to help, able to save, able to support, and simply stood idle?"

"Hardship and trials in your life were needed," Alastair replied. "Griffith, you may return to training. Anise, you and I need to sit and discuss your potential...and your future."

Alastair gave a slight wave of his arm, Griffith nodded and jogged away to another room. Alastair extended his other arm, ushering Anise over to a couch. Once she sat, Alastair pulled a chair over and sat facing her.

"Will this be a quiet place to discuss my questions?" Anise scanned the room, noting no windows or decorations but several doors.

"The doors lead where they lead," Alastair replied. "They come here when they need to, and they lead other places in times of different need."

"That's cryptic," Anise observed. "Why am I here?"

"You are a pivotal figure in the war between Heaven and Hell," Alastair began. "The Touched were created to be weapons, then angels and demons began cross-breeding with humans to create Celestials and Infernals to introduce stronger soldiers. Many humans have latent angelic or demonic ancestry within them, but only a select few can truly realize their potential."

"How am I pivotal?" Anise asked.

"You are the first to have the potential for both good and evil. Your allegiance to either side is a choice. That choice is an endorsement which carries more influence than you can even comprehend."

"Why didn't Griffith tell me this?" Anise asked. "Also, if I have both bloodlines, how am I the first? I'm simply the most recent in a string of Infernals bred with latent celestial blood."

Alastair closed his eyes for a second. When he opened them they glowed yellow and appeared unrecognizable as eyes. "Such information can never be revealed in the open. It's a matter of secrecy and security. New Celestials are brought in and exposed to their nature within these hallowed halls. I'm sure you were summoned as an Infernal too. Reactions to exposure and the repercussions vary. Controlled areas are safer for everyone. As far as your lineage, you are correct. You're not the first to have both qualities, but your connection to your stone is something none in your line have achieved. Your deeper connection to heavenly, and demonic, powers will better allow you to control both."

Anise had a puzzled look. "If I'm so pivotal, why didn't you summon me or retrieve me or whatever you call it first? Why let the Infernals bring me to them? What if I hadn't been expelled?"

"A necessary risk," he began as he stood. Alastair paced in front of Anise, his arms waved as he spoke. "Knowing you are Lilith's daughter, a premeditated approach was needed. We couldn't have you here first; it could have caused a violent reaction from the demons."

Alastair paused. His eyes returned to normal. He sat beside Anise and took her hand. "We had to gamble. I'm so sorry we allowed you to be exposed to those influences."

"What would have happened if Garrett and I hadn't exposed ourselves?" Anise asked. "If Garrett's temper hadn't driven him to his friend, and we were elsewhere when we fought those Touched, the punishment we received wouldn't have been imposed upon us."

"We observed your friend, Mr. Ladd," Alastair replied. "His temper was factored in when we made our decision to wait and retrieve you when the opportunity presented itself."

Anise's eye bulged. Her mouth gaped open. She vaulted to her feet. "What's going to happen to Garrett?"

"His destiny is his to realize," Alastair said with a dismissive wave of his hand.

"That's terrible," Anise said. "You make him sound like nothing more than a sacrificial pawn ."

"If you've received an understanding of chess, then you know a pawn's primary function is to protect a more important piece. You, Anise, are that piece. Griffith would have laid down his life bringing you to us if needed..."

"Stop!" Anise interrupted. "Just stop. If I'm so important, important enough to sacrifice strong Celestials and Infernals, important enough to be desired by Heaven and Hell, almost important enough to fight over, then why did I spend my entire life in misery?"

"All who receive great strength must be tested," Alastair replied, motioning toward the couch. "Please, sit back down."

Anise seated herself but continued to glare at Alastair. "Garrett almost died for me. I have a connection with him. Protecting me caused his quickening. He has a connection with me. It's impossible for me to simply dismiss him as inconsequential."

"He and his actions were not inconsequential," Alastair assured her. "He was an integral part of the overall chain of events."

"You still make him sound like little more than a cog in one of these factory machines, spinning for a time, then discarded when worn."

"We are all cogs in the machine of life," Alastair offered. "Some are large, some are small, but all are needed in their own way. Reproduction is the replacement of a worn cog, the analogy..."

"Wait," Anise interrupted. "Are you implying that Garrett is a worn cog past his usefulness? Are you saying I need to reproduce? What happens to Garrett now? This has all become very confusing."

Alastair raised his hand and waited for Anise to settle herself. "I mean no disrespect to your friend. His part in bringing you to us is complete, but his life has stories still to be told. He will continue in life. We will bring no harm to him."

"What about his life?" Anise asked. "He's banished from the clutch, wanted for desertion from the garrison, penniless, and now he's alone."

"At the risk of sounding callous, his situation is his to live," Alastair replied. "You need to live the life that you are uniquely capable of living."

"What am I so uniquely capable of doing?" Anise asked.

"You can bring an understanding of demonic energy to the flight for all Celestials. We can drive back the Touched and the demons. Your powers can be the shining beacon of light that ushers in a new peace; and from peace a safer world for the humans...for your friend."

"How do I do that?" Anise asked. "Why would I do that?"

"Why?" Alastair gasped. "To subdue the demons of course. To stop this endless conflict."

"Can't God stop them?" Anise questioned. "He is all-powerful."

"Your doubt wounds me, Anise," Alastair said. "God has the power, but he has never been able to bring himself to destroy his creations. God loves us all, even those who oppose him."

Anise sat in contemplative silence. Her hands ran through her hair. A tear slid down her cheek. Alastair looked on as a second tear emerged, then a third. Anise's mouth quivered and her voice shook. "Loves us all?" she said, keeping her voice low and controlled. "How does he show his love for orphans, doomed to a beggar's life? How does he show his love for prostitutes who are beaten and even murdered while trying to earn money for food? Why doesn't he help people like me? Why isn't he there for my friends? What of men like Garrett's friend John who was injured for life in a factory?"

Alastair moved over to Anise and put his hand on her shoulder. "God has said he must allow his creations to grow in their own way. Guidance is provided through the church. Punishments and rewards follow deeds, in Heaven as here on Earth."

"I've seen too much to quiet my skepticism," Anise muttered.

Alastair stood up and reached into his shirt pocket. He pulled out a necklace with a silver pendant and handed it to Anise.

Anise looked down into her hands. A pair of feathered wings sat in her palm. As she stared at them they glowed with a faint white glow. She squinted and moved her other hand to her chest. The fragment of her patron stone glowed a pale lavender. The hand with the pendant drew closer to her chest, then she moved it away.

"My patron stone must be reacting to these wings," she commented.

"The silver wings are our conduit to God's power. I have never heard of the two conduits being held by one person. The reaction between them is unknown."

"I can feel them drawing together but then pulling apart," Anise replied. "There's an attraction to a point, but then they repel."

"Your chest is glowing," Alastair said pointing. "It's a light purple. That's demonic energy!"

At the word demonic, doors sprang open. Griffith and several other Celestials burst into the room. The Celestials encircled Anise and drew their swords. An angelic yellow glow shone from their swords.

Anise howled and slammed the glowing silver wings onto her chest directly atop her patron stone fragment shining through her skin. There was a brilliant purple flash of light. Anise's wings sprouted one white batwing and one purple feathered angel wing.

"What's happening to me?" Anise screamed.

Alastair motioned for the Celestials to lower their swords. "What do you feel?" he asked. "What sensations?"

Anise's body shuddered. Her limbs shook. "I feel Lilith's power returning. My mother's energy is one with me again. My stone, it feels warm. These wings, they flutter inside me. They lift me up, somehow I feel like I'm floating even though my feet are on the ground."

"Do your wings work?" Griffith asked, lowering his sword to his side.

Anise shrugged her shoulders and let out a few grunts. She squinted and started breathing deeply. "I don't know. I'm trying. I guess, I'm consciously trying to move them, but they're still."

"Focus," Griffith coached. "What made your power emerge? What has helped you focus?"

Anise placed her hand over her chest. "I hadn't...been exposed...to anything...except this stone," she puffed out between breaths. "The demonic stone...reacted so strongly...to...to my mother's energy... in me that it fused...into my body and left me unconscious."

"Give her a moment," Alastair ordered. "Stand down, but be prepared for anything," he continued as he turned and eyed each Celestial. "Anise has the potential to be a great Celestial. We must provide our finest hospitality."

The Celestials lowered their arms. They stood rigid, swords pointed to the floor but clenched tightly in their hands.

Anise's wings began to flap. With each flap waves of energy pulsed away from her. The energy rippled out and crashed into the Celestials; many brought their arms up to protect their faces. Each ripple hit the walls with a thud, followed by a crackle.

"This power, it's, it's coursing through me," Anise gasped between wing flaps. "It feels so new, yet familiar."

Anise spun, her wings flapped, and waves of lavender light crashed into the Celestials in the room. Anise moaned, grunted, and shrieked as she twirled. The clumsy spin took on a rhythmic motion; her movements were more graceful. Her arms flowed and weaved. Even her wings went up and down in harmony. With the new rhythm, the Celestials recoiled less when impacted by the energy waves. The sound from the waves hitting the walls diminished. Revolution after revolution Anise's movements evolved into a dance. With each motion came less released energy. The light waves almost stopped. Anise crumpled to the floor. Her wings disappeared and the glow around her body dissipated.

Anise didn't move. The Celestials leaned forward and prepared their swords, some glanced at Alastair. Alastair looked around the room.

"Give her a moment," he instructed. "If she does not rise on her own, she will be taken to a room to recover."

The entire group stood silently, watching.

Griffith mouthed something, then mumbled, "Seven, eight, nine, ten..."

"What are you counting?" the Celestial beside him asked.

"How long she's been down," Griffith replied.

"Continue to count," Alastair said. "If she doesn't regain consciousness in five minutes take her somewhere to rest. Griffith, you will stand watch over her, choose someone to stand with you."

Griffith nodded. "Aileen, you will stand with me." A woman with blonde hair halfway down her back stepped forward. She wore a bright yellow dress, with her sword sheath on her back.

With Griffith and Aileen standing over Anise, the other Celestials slowly dispersed.

"You two," Alastair said pointing at the Celestials closest to Griffith. "Stay in case there is assistance required moving her. I want transitions from place to place to be gentle. The poor girl has been through so much recently."

"And not so recently," Griffith added.

As the other Celestials departed, Alastair nodded and walked through a door.

"How long has it been?" Aileen asked.

"One hundred and fifty-eight, one hundred and fifty-nine," Griffith said aloud. He stopped speaking but his eyes and lips continued to move.

Anise's body twitched and shuddered, but her eyes remained shut. She made no sounds except her laboured breathing.

Griffith counted aloud. "Two hundred and ninety-nine, three hundred. She's been down for five minutes. Time to move her. Gently everyone."

The Celestials surrounded Anise. Griffith and Aileen lifted under her shoulders. The other Celestials picked up Anise's feet. They carried her body to one of the glowing doors.

On the other side of the door was a bedroom. The walls, floor, bed, and bedding were all white with gold accents. Gingerly, they set Anise on the bed. There were four chairs in the room, each Celestial took one and moved it close to the bed. They sat in a semi-circle around the foot of the bed and watched Anise.

Chapter 16 – Trial

nise's eyes crept open. She moved her hand to her forehead. "How long?" she groaned.

"How long for what?" Aileen asked.

"How long was I unconscious?"

"We didn't track it exactly," Griffith said. "I'd approximate it to be dawn..."

"Just the night?" Anise asked using her arms to prop herself against the headboard. "That doesn't seem too bad."

"Sorry," Griffith said. "It's closer to thirty-six hours, not just overnight."

"Garrett must be worried sick," Anise blurted out. "I disappear in the middle of the night, don't return, missing an entire day and another night..." she started gasping and her voice trailed off.

Griffith stood and offered her a hand. "He should be alright."

"My concern is that he'll worry about me," Anise said. "Me being in peril caused his full powers to manifest. I fear that without the demonic energy his rage could overpower him." Anise bit her lip and gulped hard. "I shouldn't have slipped out into the night. I should have kept him aware and informed."

"You're neither his wife nor kin," Aileen said. "You're not his unless you marry."

"I need to find him," Anise insisted. "He needs to know I'm alive."

"How can he be told?" Aileen asked. "He is, or he was, or he still could be, a powerful Infernal. We can't expose him to such shocking information. His reaction could be dangerous."

"He would act to protect me," Anise argued. "I trust him, and he may need me."

Griffith offered Anise a hand. "The best way to help your friend, your town, your mortal world, is to develop your abilities. Be the light we know you can be. Place in us the same trust we placed in you."

Anise gave Griffith a blank stare. She sat still and silent. Her eyes glazed as they looked through him more than at him.

"Anise?" Griffith asked, "Are you feeling ill?"

Anise remained silent. Slowly, she shook her head from side to side. Her jaw and lower lip trembled.

"I apologize if we have upset you in some manner," Griffith said offering his hand a second time. "Please understand there are forces beyond all our comprehension involved in this war. We may never truly understand what is being asked of us. Our only possible course of action is to have faith. Submit to the light and to God, that is the world's salvation."

The door opened. From the overpowering radiance of light that poured through the doorway, Alastair emerged. "How are you feeling, Anise?"

Anise used her hand to shield her eyes from the light. "Doesn't that intense light hurt your eyes?" she asked.

"Once your abilities as a Celestial are realized the glow won't bother you," Griffith said.

"Glow?" Anise blurted out. "You call that burning, blinding, light a glow? It's more intense than staring directly at the sun on the brightest clearest of days."

Alastair's eyes narrowed. "To us, the glow is a mundane aspect of our existence. Kindly focus on your assignment."

Anise blinked. "What task have I been assigned? In addition, I have yet to confirm being recruited into your community."

Alastair stared at Anise. "The moment you took the wings and developed a glow you were one of us."

"A contract should be explained before you attempt to make it a reality," Anise replied. "I assume I can walk away and lose the ability to harness this power."

"We cannot ignore the fact you are aware of our existence and our accommodations," Alastair said.

"The light only allows those it chooses and who it deems worthy," Anise retorted. "If I were to stand with the Infernals, wouldn't your light prohibit me from entering?"

Alastair smiled. "At the very least, you pay attention. However, we expect those we bring here to become part of our flight."

"I've been subjected to a lot in my life," Anise said. "I've been abandoned, orphaned, assaulted, deceived, mistreated, summoned by trance, and now this. Forgive me, but I have great difficulty with blind trust. Call it a repercussion of the events of my life."

"Your life has been a trial," Alastair admitted. He motioned for Anise to sit back on the bed. As she sat, he joined her. He waved his arm in dismissal, but Griffith and Aileen shook their heads and stayed.

Anise shifted and squirmed on the bed. When she settled she spoke. "How has my life been a trial?"

"Your experiences, and how you handled the adverse conditions of life were how we, and the Infernals, measured your readiness," Alastair looked Anise in the eyes. He paused staring deeply into her eyes.

"What are you doing?" Anise asked with a backward lurch.

"Peering into your soul," Alastair replied. "It's a swirl of grey. No clear right or wrong. Nothing polarized about your behaviours. You are truly unique for someone with a heritage from the Heavens."

"I also have a heritage from Hell," Anise commented. "Wouldn't that cause internal turmoil? Also, you have yet to answer. Why, how has my life been some sort of trial?"

"Observe," Alastair said as he waved his arm. A cloud hovered over and shimmered. Images formed on the front of the cloud.

Anise gasped. "What is this? Some form of sorcery? Am I drugged?"

"It's a viewing portal," Griffith said.

"It allows us to see Earth, past and present," Aileen added.

"Can it see the future too?" Anise asked.

"The future is unwritten," Alastair replied.

"Doesn't God have a plan?" Anise asked with a snide grin.

"He has a plan," Alastair replied. "The plan is focused more on large events than minutia. The ends are planned, the means to those ends remain unwritten until completed."

"So, what vision is this cloud, or magic, supposed to show me?" Anise asked.

Alastair drew his sword and pointed it at the cloud. "Observe the portal," he said.

There was a slight flash. The glow on the cloud faded. An image appeared. A young girl wearing tattered rags was begging on a street corner.

A stunned look came to Anise's face. "That looks like me," she whispered. "How is this possible?"

"It is," Griffith said. "Let that be enough for now. Continue to watch and see the trials your life has actually held."

Anise stared at the images in front of her. This silent image showed a girl with her hands extended asking passersby for anything they could spare. Some showed kindness, some ignored her, and others shoved her out of their way or slapped her to the ground. Older children and teenagers passed by her. The girl in the image was shaken, beaten, thrown to the ground, kicked, and her clothing was rummaged through as those bigger than her took whatever they could find. The girl returned to her feet and her begging.

"Your determination and spirit," Alastair commented. "Even when beaten down and left with nothing you returned to your feet and continued to survive."

Anise scoffed. "What choice did I have?"

The image rippled. The background changed. The image of the young girl was replaced by an image of a baby swaddled in rags. The infant, crying, in a tattered basket was at the doorstep of a building. The door opened. A woman tried to pick up the basket, but the handle was broken on one side. The woman knelt and took the basket in her arms carrying it inside. The door closed behind her and the cloud dimmed and returned to the normal white colour.

"Abandoned, alone," Alastair began, "but you survived. Your cries alerted that woman and she took you into the orphanage. It was cold that night, had you not been heard you would have perished from exposure."

"I can't believe that some outside force was not a party in that exchange," Anise said. "If I am Lilith's daughter, bred from a demon and Infernal for generations, with a latent Celestial bloodline, meant for some higher purpose, then either you Celestials or the Infernals would have intervened. Generations of breeding, centuries of work, how can I believe all of you would abandon that? Some force other than my cries must have moved the woman to open the door."

A smirk came to Alastair's face. "As I said, large events, not minutia. The point is you survived. The woman at the orphanage opened the door and took you in." Alastair motioned back to the hovering cloud.

Lights twinkled as a new image emerged. The young girl returned to the cloud, slightly older than before. She wore the same tattered dress. Anise watched the image of the girl, standing on the street, watching older women stand in clusters on corners, men came by looking them up and down, picking through the crowd like a cattle auction. A tear came to the eye of the girl in the image as a man approached her.

Anise watched as the man touched the girl's shoulders, his eyes were seen piercing her clothes. He licked his lips, envisioning what lay beneath. Another tear came to Anise's face. "Such a barbaric act."

"Pardon me," Alastair said.

Anise tilted her head away from the cloud image. She wiped the tears from her cheek. "I called him barbaric. This was no way for young women to live."

"And, what did you do regarding the situation?" Alastair asked waving his arm.

"I learned to drug them," Anise answered. "I found a way to avoid being brutalized."

The image changed. Anise watched as a cloaked figure showed her how to grind flowers with a mortar and pestle. Mixing liquids to make the draught.

Her face turned from the cloud to Alistair. "I don't see how drugging and robbing those pathetic excuses for men constitutes an act you would hold in any positive regard."

"Your choices made the difference," Alastair said. "Watch the image. You took up the dress and demeanour of a prostitute, but you prevented adultery whenever possible. You drugged those men, you robbed them, but you never physically harmed them, and you never murdered any of them."

"So, I'm simply a lesser criminal?" Anise said with a hint of sarcasm.

"You're better than that," Griffith interrupted. "You chose to dispense justice, but you did so in a manner that allowed for a lesson instead of a death sentence."

"Griffith is correct," Alastair said. "By allowing those men to live, you allowed them a chance to improve. We believe in second chances."

Anise watched the image as a man fell unconscious and the image of her younger self rummaged through his clothing, removing coin purses, a ring, luxury items, but not his clothing, not even his prominently displayed dagger.

"I can appreciate your interpretation of these events," Anise said. "I took from them only items they could live without. My actions were less harmful than what my potential would have allowed. But what about the times when my methods didn't work? Where was my salvation then? Why didn't Griffith save me months, or even years ago? Why now? Why this instance? What's different?"

"Trials cannot be aborted during difficult circumstances," Alastair said. "Your strength can only be realized through work and suffering."

Anise shuddered and shook her head. She waved an arm through the cloud; it dissipated. "I have no desire to see or hear anymore." She lunged to her feet and stormed to the door.

"Wait," Griffith called. "We need you."

Anise ripped the door open. She spun around. "You view me as a commodity. I have dedicated my life to punishing men for acting like women are just to be bought and sold. I can't stay here." She walked through the door.

Anise entered the limbo of light. She put her arm up to block the light from her eyes. She staggered through the undefined space, one arm shielding her eyes, the other wafting and swaying in front of her searching for anything solid.

"Hello," Anise called out, her arm moving more frantically. "I'm trying to leave. I understand your entry restrictions, I know I may not be allowed to return. I still intend to go." She paused and stopped waving her arm. "I've been exposed to so much in such a short time. I need time to consider my options. I need to make the right decision. This decision cannot be rushed."

The light faded in front of Anise. She lowered her hand and saw the outline of a door. Anise crept toward the opening. She tilted her head from side to side, but there was only blinding light. She walked through the door.

Anise looked around. She was back outside, right where Griffith took her in. She patted her dress, but still no dagger, she had the coins from her attacker. Dawn was breaking.

"I wonder how long I was gone," she mumbled to herself. She started walking, back into the Old Quarter. As she walked, she continued to mumble, "Angel or demon, light or dark, Garrett, Thraz, Alastair, Griffith, Roven, Calypso, Aileen...so many new people, or whatever they are. So many factors to consider. What do I do? How do I choose?"

Anise's eyelids drooped, she raised her hand to her mouth and tried to stifle the yawn. She rubbed her eyes and plodded through the streets. The mumbling continued at an almost silent level. "Light...dark...Heaven...Hell..." When Anise stopped mumbling she looked up. In front of her was the abandoned house she and Garrett had been living in. She went inside.

Anise found Garrett in the main room. He was sitting by the hearth, watching the fire, and twisting Anise's dagger in his hands.

"How long was I gone?" Anise asked.

Garrett jumped to his feet, pointing the dagger toward Anise. His eyes widened, he lowered the dagger, turned its handle toward Anise and offered it to her. "Three days."

Anise took her dagger and sheathed it. "Thank you."

"What happened to you?" Garrett asked.

"It's a long story," Anise answered. "The most important aspect, which is also the most difficult, is that I'm part Infernal, part Celestial, capable of being either, and I have an enormous decision to make."

"Unbelievable," Garrett said, putting his hands on his knees and sitting back in front of the fire. "Yet, somehow not."

"I was taken to a flight," Anise replied. "It's their version of a clutch. I have silver wings. I even manifested a different form, angelic and demonic."

"You're back here," Garrett observed. "Did you choose me? Us?"

"Nothing is finalized," Anise answered. "Now, what I need is sleep." She curled up in a blanket in front of the fire. Garrett slid over beside her, watching as she slept.

Chapter 17 – Decision

By the fire, Garrett hunched over, watching Anise as she slept. His eyes trained on her, he observed her breathing. He only turned away to add wood to the fire. Occasionally he looked at the shaft of light coming through the window, noting the passage of time as it crossed the floor.

The shaft of light reached the far end of the room. Daylight dimmed to dusk. Anise stirred. Slowly, she sat up. She looked at Garrett. "How long was I asleep?"

"Almost the entire day," he replied. "The sun's setting. You must've been exhausted. What happened?"

"I went out," Anise started. "I made the drug, I was trying to get some coin for food. The man didn't want a drink, he didn't want anything but his lust fulfilled." She paused and looked toward the fire. Garrett turned, the flame was dimming, he added two more pieces of wood. "Where did you get the wood?"

"I sold the rabbit pelts and managed to catch and sell a few more while you were gone. Tell me the rest. What happened to you?"

"The man attacked me. Then another man appeared. A Celestial. He brought me to their flight, much like we brought Roven and others to the clutch. I reacted to their silver wings, their channelling focus. They showed me how my past was a trial. They've been watching everything to determine my worth. I reacted to my stone again as well. I could feel both energies inside me, mingling..." she stopped and stood up. She paced around the room.

"What's the matter?" Garrett asked.

"I have to make a choice," Anise replied. "Am I a Celestial or an Infernal? Am I somehow both? Which world do I belong to?"

"That is a question beyond anything I could answer," Garrett replied. "How can anyone make such a choice? It's like there's no suitable option."

"They made me feel like a commodity," Anise said. "To them, I'm little more than a chess piece in their game. They were watching my whole life, yet they didn't intervene until I was of value. Where were they when I was beaten before? Where were they when I was growing up alone? What did they do for me?"

Garrett intercepted her pacing and wrapped his arm around Anise. "How could they? Much like the Infernal world, until your powers were ready to manifest there was little to be done. Secret societies measure risk against reward. I know that's of little to no comfort. It pains me to say it. There was no joy living the experience."

Anise pouted and shrugged Garrett's arm off her. "You make it sound like I was left alone, abandoned, abused, and assaulted because of basic arithmetic. I would have preferred compassion before mathematics. What if I had died before my powers came out? What about the centuries of breeding to make me what I am?"

"I was watching you," Garrett said. "I was to observe and only act if you were in mortal danger. I'm sorry I couldn't have intervened; it pained me greatly on many occasions. I suppose that's why I watch over you as I do now."

"How old are you, Garrett?"

"I'm thirty."

"How long did you watch me before I was summoned?"

Garrett looked away, clenching his lips. "Five years."

They sat and stared at each other in silence. A minute passed. The silence was broken by a growl from Anise's stomach.

"There isn't any food ready," Garrett said. "I ate what little I could afford yesterday after securing the wood. The nights are getting colder as autumn approaches."

Anise reached under her dress. She pulled out the coin pouches from her attacker. "When the Celestial saved me, I took coin pouches from my attacker before he fled. We should see if any markets are still open."

"It will be dark soon," Garrett said. "It's best if we hurry."

Gathering their burlap bags, they hustled down the streets to the Exchange.

Panting from their rush, Anise and Garrett entered the Exchange. Very few food vendors and farmers were still there, and most of the merchants with general goods were already gone. The rows and rows of tables were almost bare. Garrett and Anise trudged across the dirt floor surveying the remaining wares. One vendor was left with bruised produce. Garrett inspected a few pieces.

"I'll give you a copper for three of these apples," he offered.

The man looked away for a moment, then looked up to meet Garrett's eyes. "If you have two copper you may have five," the man said.

Garrett scoured the table, he handled almost every apple, setting aside the ones he saw fit. "Deal." He reached out to Anise. She pulled out a coin purse and rummaged through it. Anise handed Garrett two copper coins. Garrett set them on the table and bagged the apples.

"Pleasure doing business with you," the man said. "Come again. Come early, I'll have finer fruit."

Garrett nodded and walked away. He approached another table with Anise a step behind. The baker had very few loaves of bread left. Garrett began squeezing them.

"These feel firm, how old are they?" he asked.

The baker replied with an indignant glare. "Baked this morning, but they've been sitting here all day."

Garrett wiped some dust from the loaf in his hand. "Fairly dusty for one day. Are you sure they haven't sat longer?"

"No need for insolence," the baker snapped. "Today has been especially dry, dust has been stirred up from the floor. Nothing more to say than that."

"I'll give you a copper for two of them," Anise offered with an extended hand presenting the coin.

The baker's mouth scrunched. "It's late, I'll accept your offer." She snatched the coin from Anise and quickly stuffed it into the pocket of her apron.

Garrett and Anise picked up their bread and walked away down the row of tables. The bustling sounds of commerce were much quieter than the morning. Few barkers were announcing their wares, and children no longer played in the aisles as their mothers shopped.

"You rushed that," Garrett said nodding his head toward the baker's table.

"I wanted to avoid an altercation," Anise sighed. "I'm tired, hungry, and I wish to keep what composure I have until we get back to the house."

Garrett walked ahead, his eyes darting from table to table looking for anything else to purchase. "I don't know what we are even going to be able to eat tonight."

"Hard bread and apples it would seem," Anise replied. "Not fit for royalty but fit for us."

Garrett grumbled something indistinguishable as he plodded along through a row of empty tables. His feet scraped the dirt floor with a grinding noise. The dust was stirred to knee height. At the end of the row, another farmer was packing up his table.

"Do you still have wares to sell?" Garrett asked.

"I have a couple bunches of carrots," the man replied looking into the cart he was packing. He pulled out two bunches of carrots tied with string. He set the carrots on the table and started to rummage. "Empty sack, empty sack, empty sack, ah yes, I have four potatoes left."

"How much for all of it?" Garrett asked.

"Three copper pennies," the farmer replied.

Anise fished through the coin purse. "Do you have change for a tin chit? I only see two copper in here."

The farmer nodded. He opened his coin pouch and retrieved two pennies. Anise exchanged the tin for copper as Garrett bagged the carrots and potatoes.

"We should go," Anise said. "We have enough for tonight."

Garrett closed the sack of food and started toward the exit. Anise followed at a quick step and slowed to walk beside him. They went out into the street. The lamplighter's boots clicked on the stone as he lit the lamps along the road. The sun was almost completely set and the roads were bare. Anise and Garrett headed toward the house.

Garrett stopped. He lifted his heel and twisted the ball of his foot on the road. "Anise, may I ask you something?"

"So formal. Ask."

"Have you any idea how you'll decide between Infernal and Celestial?" he asked.

"Sadly, I have no idea," Anise replied. "The silver wings, the patron stone, they both resonate when I hold them. My stone fused with me, and Lilith is my mother. Infernals brought me in and gave me a home. The Celestials speak of me as a weapon, as a commodity, as cattle. But can I be *evil* as an Infernal? Can I serve and tie myself to Hell?"

As Anise finished the question, there was a groaning noise from behind. Anise and Garrett spun around. Two Shamblers emerged from an alley a few houses away. They shuffled toward Anise and Garrett. The Shamblers scuffed the ground with their feet. They lumbered forward, arms raised reaching ahead. Garrett drew his spear and extended it.

"Get behind me," he ordered.

"You don't have your DHEC energy, that spear won't be any use," Anise argued. "We can outrun them. Let's go."

Anise started to run. Garrett jogged backwards, then turned and quickened his pace to catch Anise. A block down the street Anise tripped. Garrett pulled her to her feet.

"Ow!" Anise exclaimed. "My ankle, it hurts. I don't know if I can walk."

Garrett looked behind him. The Shamblers were still in pursuit. He pulled her arm over his shoulders. Anise hopped and hobbled. Garrett adjusted his pace. Beads of sweat formed on Garrett's forehead and ran down his face. He panted and huffed hustling past the abandoned buildings in the Old Quarter. Their pace was slower than the Shamblers. The gap narrowed.

Anise looked back and stopped hopping. "You need to save yourself. You can't protect me from them, and you can't escape helping me."

"What...what would...you...have me do?" Garrett puffed out. "I refuse, to abandon you."

Garrett heaved his shoulders to refresh his hold of Anise's arm. He faced forward. The sweat glistened in the light of the streetlamps as it slid down his cheek. Each step was a huff, deeper and deeper breathing, followed by grunts. After four blocks Garrett stopped and Anise slid away from him, putting her full weight on her feet. She crumpled to the ground. Garrett dropped to his knees beside her. He looked back. The Shamblers drew closer.

"Now we're both in danger," Anise said. "Hopefully some Infernal or Celestial is nearby and sees value in rescuing me."

"I doubt fortune will smile on us," Garrett said standing up. He steadied himself and readied his spear. He took a step toward the Shamblers, covering Anise.

She tugged on his pant leg. "You don't stand a chance. Go!"

Garrett brushed her hand away and staggered toward the approaching Shamblers. He jabbed his spear into the shoulder of one and pulled it back. Ichor came from the wound. The Shambler continued forward. It lunged forward clubbing Garrett with its arm. Garrett tumbled to the ground, raised himself to one knee and thrust his spear forward. He stabbed the Shambler in the stomach. Ichor ran down the spear shaft. The Shambler grabbed the spear and wrestled for control. Garrett struggled to maintain his grip but failed. The Shambler flung the spear away, it clinked and clattered as it rolled to a stop on the stone street. Garrett hopped back and dove for his spear.

"Garrett!" Anise screamed as the Shambler's arm swung at him. "Get away!"

Garrett had little time to recover, two more Shamblers approached from an alley two blocks away. Garrett whirled around. He saw four Shamblers and Anise crumpled on the ground working to rise to her knees. The injured Shambler backed away. The other three passed Anise and circled Garrett. He spun, jabbed his spear, and swung wildly, but the Shamblers continued to approach. Garrett's chest heaved with each breath. He grunted with each thrust and swing of his spear. The Shambler's arms swung like clubs. Garrett raised his arms and spear. He deflected some blows. He sidestepped others and took only glancing impacts to his arms. Garrett's grunts and groans from the beating blended with the moaning noises made by the Shamblers as they swung. Garrett's stomach growled. One hand instinctively covered it. A Shambler's arm bashed Garrett's head. He shuffled away and readied his spear, jabbing forward. The Shamblers stayed at a distance. One approached and Garrett jabbed. The others tried to advance, but Garrett's spear moved quickly enough to keep them at bay. Garrett tried to thrust his body up. His knee lifted off the ground and dropped back immediately.

"Stop!" Anise shouted, trying to stand. "Leave him alone!"

One Shambler stepped back from Garrett and shuffled toward Anise. It moaned out the words, "quiet, you are next," as it narrowed the gap.

"Anise!" Garrett yelled. "Get away from here."

"I can't abandon you," she protested. "You're the best person I've known my whole life." A tear came to her eye and rolled down her cheek. "For the first time I've had the ability to do great things, and now I'm reduced to being unable to walk and I'm about to be turned by an abomination. I'm so frustrated I want to scream."

"Scream," Garrett called back while bobbing and blocking attacks. "Maybe someone will hear you." With each step he took, the Shamblers adjusted their positions. They kept him surrounded.

Anise's head tilted back. Tears ran from her eyes along her cheekbones to her earlobes. Her eyes opened and closed as she let out a screeching howl.

The stone in her chest pulsed. A purple light blinked through her dress. Her skin changed colour and her aura engulfed her body. Her wings crept from her shoulders and stretched. Her eyes glowed purple.

Anise cackled with glee. She flapped her wings and floated to her feet. Her aura whip manifested and crackled in her hand. She drew her dagger and ran her aura through the blade.

The Shambler stopped approaching. While it paused, Anise took advantage. She lashed her whip at the Shambler, wrapping the whip around the creature's neck. She flew forward and buried her dagger in the Shambler's chest. The beast groaned and gagged as her aura coursed through its body. Anise ripped the blade out and watched the ichor ooze from the wound. With her good foot, she kicked the Shambler to the ground. It writhed and twitched with both arms over the opening in its chest, choking and coughing up more ooze.

Anise took flight, soaring toward Garrett and the three Shamblers stomping on him. She sailed by, burying her dagger in a Shambler's neck on the first pass. She swung around sharply for another attack. Her whip wrapped around the second Shambler's legs. She flew past and dragged the beast away from Garrett. It screamed foul guttural noises as it bounced off the uneven stones in the street.

Garrett rolled away from the final Shambler. He struggled to his knees. He held his stomach as sweat and tears soaked his face. His skin was bruised and discoloured, and his left eye swollen shut.

"Ah-Anise," he coughed out. "What's happening?"

Anise released her aura whip and swooped in between Garrett and the last Shambler. The creature slowed its pursuit of the injured Garrett and stared at Anise. As the aura whip released and the purple crackle dissipated the battered Shambler came to its feet. Slowly, it crept to join its uninjured ally.

Anise stood steady between the Shamblers and Garrett. She reached for her dagger. A momentary quirk of her face happened when her hand reached the empty scabbard. She looked over to the Shambler on the ground with the dagger handle sticking out from its neck. She hummed and her eyes fluttered. Aura whips crackled and glistened as they emerged from both her hands.

She glanced over her shoulder at Garrett. "I'll protect you."

He managed to have one foot flat on the ground and was pressing his knee with both hands in an attempt to stand. "How? How do you have your aura and DHEC energy back?"

Anise stepped back, closer to Garrett. Her voice was clear, her movements deliberate as she narrowed the gap between them. "Much like your quickening, a cherished friend in danger forced open the pathways we channel the DHEC through."

Garrett reached out. His fingers grazed the back of Anise's knee. Her purple aura flowed down his arm and sheathed his body in the crackling lavender light.

"I feel the DHEC!" Garrett exclaimed. "I feel it, coursing through my arm, my body, my legs." His arms and legs moved freely as he regained his feet. The purple glow around him was bled with blue; Garrett was sheathed in red. His eyes glowed orange, his feathered wings sprouted from his back. The red glow dimmed to orange. Garrett drew his spear. It was bathed in shining orange light. He flapped his wings and floated beside Anise. He looked over and smiled, "thank you."

Chapter 18 - Reawakening

nise floated aside. She winked at Garrett. "These two are yours if you wish. I was able to revisit my abilities, it's your turn."

Smiling, he twirled the spear in his hands. Garrett sprang forward, thrusting his spear into the uninjured Shambler. The creature howled as the orange aura forced through its body and burst out its back. Garrett planted his feet on the ground and forced himself back. He flew away and the Shambler fell to the ground. "That was a wonderful feeling."

"You look your old self," Anise replied. "Our demonic heritage has been restored and so has our healing." She set herself on the ground and walked to the dead Shambler to retrieve her dagger. "My ankle is of no further concern."

"I no longer feel pain from the bruising," Garrett commented. "Now to see what I can really channel." His eyes fluttered and he hummed, his body shuddered and his wings twitched. Garrett allowed his spear to retract. He placed both hands on the hilt. Garrett's aura grew from the handle. The orange light formed a blade wreathed in flames. Garrett walked with purpose toward the remaining Shambler.

"Deceitful Infernals," the Shambler groaned. "You trap our kind to exterminate."

Garrett stomped the few last steps, whirling his aura blade in revolutions above his head increasing in speed. He stopped short of the Shambler and straightened his arms for the final round of the blade. The blade cleaved the Shambler's head from its shoulders. The body fell to its knees and then forward to the ground. The head landed near the body, rolled a few feet, then came to a stop. Garrett stared into the beast's dead eyes.

"I wonder what he meant by exterminate," Anise commented, sheathing her dagger.

Garrett's head rose. He walked over to Anise, dismissing his sword and sheathing the spear handle. "I never thought about it. I suppose to them we're perceived as hunters."

"Could we really be hunters?" Anise asked. "I always viewed our role as that of a protector."

They released their auras. Anise cried out, grabbing her ankle, and fell into a heap on the ground. "My ankle," she gasped, holding her foot.

Garrett groaned. "As soon as I released my aura...the pain from their barrage returned." He coughed.

"We should return to the house," Anise said. "Let's collect our meagre food supply and recover."

Garrett nodded. "Agreed. We could be quicker if we used the DHEC again, but that could attract unwanted attention."

"Now that we can channel demonic energy again we also need to discuss our options," Anise added.

Garrett picked up the bags from the Exchange and helped Anise to her feet. Using Garrett for stability, she managed to walk back to the abandoned house. Garrett settled her on the floor and rebuilt the fire in the hearth.

"Wood is low," Garrett said. "I'll replenish our supply tomorrow."

"The tattered blankets and a small fire will keep us warm enough," Anise assured him. "The weather is still mild enough for comfort."

Garrett lit the fire and warmed up what little food was available. "We should eat, and then rest."

Anise nodded. "Your bruises will be sore for some time, so will my ankle; it's swelling." Anise removed her shoe. The ankle was a deep purple colour and twice the size of her other ankle.

Garrett blinked and looked her in the eye. "You'll receive no argument from me. I've seen ankles like that before as a soldier. You should stay off it for several days, maybe even a week."

Anise let out a huff. "An entire week?" She rubbed the ankle and looked at Garrett with despair. "We need our demonic healing returned."

"We have no idea whether we can channel again or not," Garrett said. "We were in extreme danger and you managed to force a connection, but how? How do we do that again?"

Anise stared at her ankle. "I suppose I'm being unreasonable. We also have no clutch, no assistance, and no home beyond this decrepit abandoned building." She pounded her fist on the floor.

Garrett brought her a bowl of food. "Eat something; perhaps a full stomach will improve your outlook." He sat beside her and started eating. Between bites, Garrett flashed a kind smile.

Anise accepted the bowl but set it down. "I have no appetite. The food is appealing; I just have no hunger or desire to eat. I'm sorry."

"I haven't any appetite either," Garrett commented. "I thought perhaps it was because of my disgust with our situation, but now, I wonder if our brief experience with the DHEC has replenished us as it once did."

"We felt healed," Anise added. "It is reasonable to assume the DHEC energy has filled our stomachs as well. Save the food, we shall see how we feel in the morning."

"The healing didn't last long," Garrett sighed. "Hopefully the hunger will be staved off longer than the pain was."

Garrett draped a blanket over Anise and sat beside her. "Hopefully the DHEC will leave some residual healing and we will recover by morning. Tonight, we should remain here, keep warm, and rest." Garrett stood up, piled what little wood was left within arms reach and reseated himself beside Anise.

Anise shivered as he sat down. "Throw another piece of wood on the fire, please."

Garrett complied. He lobbed a club-sized branch into the hearth. It crackled as it lit the room. Anise crossed her arms and rubbed her upper arms. The shivering subsided. She leaned against Garrett and breathed a sigh of comfort.

They sat together watching the flickers of light dance in the fireplace. Garrett occasionally tossed an extra branch in. There was silence in the room, stillness, peace. Anise's eyes grew weary, her eyelids sagged and reopened.

"Did you hear that?" Anise whispered with a gasp.

Garrett tilted his head slightly. "Hear what?"

Anise kept her body still as her hand crept toward her dagger. "A scraping noise, like someone dragging their feet."

"You think some Shamblers may have tracked us here?" Garrett asked reaching for his spear handle.

"I don't believe so," Anise replied clutching her dagger handle and leaning slightly away from Garrett. "It was brief, a single scuff, Shamblers would continue to scrape the ground and we would hear more."

Garrett's gaze crept around the room. He moved his shoulder and added to his range while feigning a stretch. The stretching motion moved him far enough from Anise, she was able to adjust her legs from crossed to bent together under her.

"I'm ready if I need to pounce," she whispered.

"I haven't seen anything yet," Garrett breathed out while trying to hold his lips still. "I need to end this stretch motion soon or anyone spying on us will become suspicious."

"Behave as though you heard nothing," Anise advised. "I'm going to stand up, get some food for you, and then go to the other room. That may allow me to see who or what is out there."

Anise crawled to her knees and stood up. She filled a bowl from the pot on the fire and handed it to Garrett. Anise stretched her arms and legs and hobbled around the room. Each step made her wince. She walked to the smaller rooms, waited at the outside wall with her head cocked and her ear cupped in her hand and walked back to Garrett. "I saw nothing. No noises either."

Garrett stood as Anise sat. "More wood in the other room." He placed a branch from the pile on the fire and walked out. Garrett shifted his eyes from side to side as he walked. He went to the backroom and collected what loose boards, sticks, and other shattered wood he could scrape together. He returned to the main room, added his armload to the pile and sat with his bowl. "No sightings."

They rearranged their blankets and huddled together in the glow of the fire. "I saw some actual logs in there," Garrett said. "They were behind the broken boards and sticks. We should have wood for another day, possibly two."

Anise nodded. "At least we have some positive news."

They sat in silence. Garrett added another couple of pieces of wood to the fire.

"I heard something," Anise hissed.

"What was it?" Garrett whispered.

"Another scraping noise," Anise whispered back. "I wouldn't be surprised if someone or something is outside."

"Another? Or the same source as the last sound?" Garrett said in muffled grunts.

Anise looked at the fire intently. "The same, or very similar."

"Keep your focus on the fire," Garrett mumbled. He stood and spoke normally. "I should fetch more wood from the other room."

Garrett walked to the smaller room, he returned with an armful of split logs. "This should make an adequate pile." He set the logs on the floor. While seating himself Garrett leaned toward Anise and whispered, "I thought I heard a slight noise, but I'm not certain what it was."

"I don't feel comfortable sleeping with some prowler outside," Anise whispered. "If it's some form of Touched, how do we proceed?"

Garrett stood up and grasped his spear. "This is becoming more stressful than it should be. I'm going to check outside and see what the source of the noise is."

Battered as he was, Garrett crept cautiously to the door. His steps were uneven. At times he grasped his side with his empty hand. Anise's eyes watered as she watched him cross the room and open the door.

Garrett stepped outside and closed the door behind him. He looked left and right down the street. Before him was nothing more than empty cobblestone streets, dimly lit by the flickers of the streetlamps. There was a clattering noise in the alley. Garrett extended his spear and crept around the corner. "Who's down there?"

There was a rustling noise. A figure emerged in the dark. Slowly, a man approached Garrett. Garrett readied his spear. "Identify yourself!"

"It's me, Roven," replied a familiar voice.

Garrett relaxed his grip on the spear and backed into the street. As Roven approached the street, the candles from the streetlights illuminated his face.

"Why are you here?" Garrett asked.

"Thraz sent me," Roven replied. "Alessa, the clairvoyant, sensed a tremendous amount of DHEC energy being channelled in this area. We knew of no Infernal on patrol, so I was dispatched to investigate."

"Anise and I have been squatting here since we were banished," Garrett said. "We were attacked by Shamblers. Somehow our powers were forced awake again."

Roven's head twitched, his eyes bulged. "That's amazing. How is Anise?"

Garrett motioned toward the door. "Come inside. We can speak there. There's no need to stand out in the cold."

They went inside. Anise smiled at the sight of Roven. "Hello, Roven. I'm glad it's you and not some Shamblers."

"Thank you," Roven said. "It's good to see you two are surviving." Roven's hands twitched. He looked around avoiding eye contact with Anise or Garrett.

"Is something troubling you?" Anise asked.

"My orders," Roven answered. "They've become...unclear."

"How so?" Garrett asked placing a piece of broken board on the fire.

"My instructions were to return to the clutch with whatever person was the source of the DHEC energy Aleesa sensed," Roven confessed. "However, we also have orders to avoid any association with the two of you. Your banishment is being treated as ex-communication. I don't know which order overrides the other."

Anise looked at him. "Our powers have returned. If we were truly meant to be excommunicated, surely we would have been left for dead instead of being granted the power to defend ourselves."

"Very true," Roven said, stroking his chin. "If the Patron Stone has allowed DHEC energy to flow to you there must have been a reason the lords of Hell allowed it."

"What were your orders?" Garrett asked. "Are you to report your findings, or bring in the Infernals responsible for the unknown energy?"

Roven looked around the room. He stared at the fire silently.

"Roven?" Anise called. He looked over. "What were your orders? You focused on the fire and failed to answer Garrett."

"I'm to report my findings," Roven said. His eyes shifted as he spoke.

"You're avoiding eye contact," Anise observed. "Is there something else you aren't telling us?"

Roven glanced at his feet and mumbled, "I lied."

"Timid as ever," Garrett chided.

"Garrett," Anise scolded.

"Lied about what?" Garrett insisted. "What are you trying to hide from us?"

Roven looked up. He burst out, "I'm afraid!"

"Afraid of what?" Anise asked.

"About bringing you two back, about even being in contact with you," he replied. Roven started wringing his hands and rolling them together. "When you were banished, we were told you were off limits. Contact with you is a punishable offence. Here I am, in your new home, being warmed by your fire. How will Thraz react?"

Garrett put his hand on Roven's shoulder. "We should all return to the clutch. The return of our abilities is a sign. We have reawakened. We should go home."

"Test your abilities," Roven said. "I'm trembling inside from the nervous feeling being in your presence gives me. I need to be certain."

Anise climbed to her feet. She squealed and winced when she put weight on her ankle. Garrett stabilized her. They both began to hum and their bodies shuddered. The purple and orange auras appeared. Wings sprouted. The pigmentation of their skin changed.

Roven stared silently for a moment, then lunged forward and hugged both Anise and Garrett. The three crashed to the floor in a heap. "I missed you," Roven said, picking himself up.

Garrett and Anise looked at one another, chuckled, and stood up.

"We should watch that fire until it burns out," Garrett said. "Even in a stone fireplace sparks could be thrown and ignite nearby wood."

"We could douse it," Anise offered. "We have a bucket of water."

Garrett sighed. "I would rather the hearth was dry, as a precaution. If Thraz rejects our return, we will remain in exile. If we're still exiled, we're sleeping here. If forced to stay here, I'd prefer to stay warm."

Anise nodded. "That's a wise decision. I assumed we would be accepted back into the clutch. This is our contingency plan."

"You two should dismiss your auras," Roven said. "We don't want to attract attention."

Anise nodded. She dismissed her aura. Once the aura faded, she fell and grabbed her ankle. "I'm going to need help walking."

Garrett released his aura and helped Anise to her feet. He let out a grunt. "The DHEC healing is quite helpful for pain, but undesirable attention is the greater of the two concerns."

They watched as the fire dwindled to embers. As the crackling noises subsided and the flames faded the three prepared to leave.

Roven walked into the street followed by Garrett, supporting Anise. The walk through the streets was slow; Roven frequently paused while Garrett and Anise caught up.

"Sorry I'm going too fast," Roven said.

"You're trying to return home and avoid an incident," Anise panted. "We understand."

Block after block they struggled. Garrett's face was flushed and sweaty. Even with weight on Garrett instead of her ankle Anise hissed out muffled noises almost every step.

They approached the warehouse. There was a refreshing breeze. Everyone inhaled deeply. Roven proceeded to open the door. He held it for Anise and Garrett as they hobbled through.

Inside, familiar sights and sounds greeted them. Barrels and tables, training dummies being used by other Infernals, the clanging of steel on steel, and Thraz's voice providing direction where he saw fit.

Within moments there was a hush, broken only by whispers and hissing noises.

Thraz stormed across the room. "What are they doing here?"

Roven trembled as his eyes met Thraz's. "They're the source of the DHEC energy Aleesa sensed."

"How is that possible?" Thraz demanded. "They were banished and the Patron Stone disconnected them from the DHEC."

Anise and Garrett met eyes and nodded. They hummed and their eyes fluttered. The purple and orange auras surrounded them.

"We were attacked," Anise said. "Shamblers came at us and we were in a desperate situation. Somehow the barriers preventing our stones from channelling energy were broken down."

"Anise saved me," Garrett said. "Her energy came first, then it activated mine. We're uncertain of any specifics, but extreme peril is the most likely cause."

"Your expulsion was ordered from above me," Thraz said. "If the Stone, or some greater demon's intervention, has allowed a reawakening there must be a reason. If they have reason, I wish I knew whether or not to welcome you back to the clutch."

"Our powers saved us," Anise said. "If demonic power saved us, then someone wants us alive."

"The question is why?" Thraz replied. "If a demon has a plan for you, it doesn't mean they want you back here. They might want to kill you on their own terms."

Garrett put his hand on Thraz's shoulder. "Alessa sensed us. Roven found us. Some power empowered us. Everything that happened today played out like there was a plan to return us to the clutch."

Thraz huffed. "How can I be certain?"

"What blocked our access to the DHEC?" Anise asked. "We were punished for revealing ourselves."

"And danger forced your powers awake before," Thraz added.

"Perhaps our mortal terror reawakened our Infernal abilities," Anise offered.

Thraz scowled. "Is that your contention? The danger you were in overrode the Stone punishing you? The sheer unmitigated self-importance. How can you believe you're stronger than the Stone? How can you believe you're beyond the control of the lords of Hell?"

"Exactly!" Anise exclaimed. "How could we be so strong? How could we override whatever power blocked our access to the DHEC? We were granted our powers to preserve our lives. Whoever made that decision has a plan for us, wants us."

Thraz bit his lip. "I have my concerns, but you'll be allowed to return, provisionally. You'll be under observation and you're not being assigned any missions alone."

"Thank you," Garrett said.

Thraz turned. "Everyone, Anise and Garrett have reawakened. They are Infernals once more. We welcome them home. Once they have had sufficient rest they'll return to active duty."

Anise looked around to see smiling faces, applause, and cheering within the warehouse. She smiled as a tear came to her eye.

Garrett stepped forward. "Thank you all for the warm welcome. It has been a difficult few days. We're elated to be home and receive such a wonderful reception. We should rest. The rest of you, back to training."

The cheers stopped. The crowd stared at Garrett. Thraz stepped up beside Garrett and placed a hand on his shoulder.

"Well said," Thraz said to Garrett. Thraz looked up. "The rest of you heard him, back to your training!"

The Infernals returned to sparring and working with the dummies. Anise and Garrett headed for small rooms to find a place to sleep.

Chapter 19 – Calling

nise woke. Lying still, she scanned the storage room. It was empty except for Garrett, who sat on a barrel beside her.

"How long did we sleep?" Anise asked.

"I was told I slept for a whole day," Garrett replied. "I've been sitting here waiting for you to wake up for an entire day."

"I slept for two days?" Anise asked with a blink.

Garrett nodded. "Aleesa and Thraz want to see us both. They said they would wait for you to wake on your own."

Anise stood up. She patted down her clothing, confirming she still had her dagger. "Let's not keep them waiting any longer than necessary."

Anise walked into the main room with Garrett right behind. Anise surveyed the room. It was the typical sight, some Infernals training, some channelling DHEC auras, a few sitting and tending to their equipment.

"The main room is busy as always," Anise commented. "I haven't spotted Thraz yet. Do you see him, Garrett?"

Garrett looked from left to right. "No. It's peculiar he's not observing or instructing someone."

Anise scanned the room again. "I don't see Aleesa either. I wonder where they are."

"Behind you," Thraz said.

Anise jumped. Garrett spun around. Thraz and Aleesa stood behind them.

Aleesa motioned for Anise and Garrett to go back inside the small room. "We should speak in private."

They sat on crates and Thraz moved a barrel in front of the door to block it.

"You're wondering why we've been so secretive," Aleesa said. "Sadly, I don't have all the answers you seek. None of us truly know how or why you were able to reawaken your powers. It has never happened before."

Anise stared at Aleesa. "What do you know?"

"We know you somehow reawakened," Thraz barked. "We've been trying to commune with our contacts in hopes of an audience with a greater demon to make inquiries. Thus far, no replies."

"Are we in some sort of suspension or limbo?" Garrett asked. "Are we to return to duty? Or are we on standby until this is resolved?"

Aleesa sighed. "We don't have a suitable answer. There are still too many unknowns. What exactly happened when you reawakened?"

"We were attacked," Anise said. "There were three Shamblers. I tripped and hurt my ankle. It was hard to stand. Garrett tried to take my weight and help me, but we moved too slow to escape. He tried fighting them. The Shambler knocked him to the ground and the group stomped on him. I feared for his life, and for my own. Suddenly my aura manifested. I felt the DHEC again. It flowed through me like it never left."

"She reached out to me," Garrett added. "I felt her energy pass to me. My body drew her energy in and used it."

Thraz and Aleesa exchanged glances. "Did anything else unusual happen while you were banished?"Aleesa asked.

Anise took a deep breath. "I know the truth."

Thraz's eyes narrowed. He glared at Anise. "What truth?"

"That I was bred to be a weapon. I am a hybrid with demonic and angelic bloodlines," Anise replied.

The room went silent.

"I went out to revisit my old ways. I was attacked, beaten, and unable to stop the man. Someone intervened. A Celestial. He brought me to their flight. It was revealed to me that I have the potential to be either Infernal or Celestial. They tried to recruit me."

"Recruit you?" Aleesa repeated.

Anise stared at the floor. "They told me they watched me my whole life. They let me suffer. They allowed my childhood to be as brutal as it was. They were idle while I was abused. When I asked why, all they had to say was they were testing me."

Anise trembled. Garrett placed a hand on her shoulder. "I'll go with you."

"They waited to create a creature with both demonic and angelic properties." A tear rolled down her cheek.

Garrett put his hand on Anise's shoulder. "We're here for you. I'm here for you."

"Perhaps your ability to tap into the angelic bloodline's power created a new path for DHEC energy to flow," Thraz said.

Aleesa's voice changed. Her eyes glowed red. "Anise Lovejoy, you are summoned. A transit gate will be provided. Enter it." Each statement was direct and authoritarian.

Aleesa waved her hands. The crimson glow wafted from her eyes, billowing like smoke as she twisted her arms. The red smoke swirled in front of Anise. The pattern looked random, but the smoke formed a shape. An arched doorway appeared before Anise. There was no wood, no steel, no solid surface. Swirling trails of red light flowed within the archway. White smoke emanated from the centre, wafting out in all directions. While the lights remained confined to the interior of the archway, the smoke crept out into the room.

"Enter it," the voice from Aleesa repeated.

"ENTER!" the voice possessing Aleesa boomed.

Anise took a step forward, her leg shook through the entire motion. Garrett kept pace.

"A summons is best answered promptly," Thraz said. "It can be very intimidating, but you must face it directly."

"You've never spoken kinder words to me," Anise gasped. Another tear rolled down her face. "Thank you."

Anise stepped up to the swirling image and placed her hand on the surface of the portal. Her hand disappeared as it passed through the gateway. "It feels warm, hot even, but somehow familiar and welcoming."

"That's hellfire," Thraz commented. "You will feel sweltering heat, but there shouldn't be any discomfort because that is the environment your demon side is native to."

Garrett put his hand to the gate. "We can enter together."

"ENTER!" the voice from Aleesa boomed.

Anise inhaled deeply and stepped forward. Garrett followed. The swirling mist in the portal rippled around them. Their bodies disappeared.

"I hope they fare well," Alessa said in her normal voice.

Thraz grumbled something indistinguishable and trudged back to the training room.

Chapter 20 - Meeting

nise emerged from the wafting crimson portal, stopping only two steps from the portal to take in her surroundings. Garrett stepped through behind her. Placing his hands on her shoulders, he nudged her forward and assessed the area for potential threats. The chamber they entered was hot, but they didn't sweat. Fires burning in ponds of red ooze lit the room. Rough gray stone with splashes of rust brown made up the walls and floor.

"This looks like some sort of cavern," Anise commented.

"Where do you suppose the party meant to greet us is hiding?" Garrett asked. "You've been summoned to what appears to be an empty room."

Anise clutched her chest. The light from her stone fragment pulsed brightly through her dress, illuminating the room more than the fires. There was a silver streak in the lilac light.

"Your stone?" Garrett gasped. "What's happening with it?"

"I...I don't know," Anise panted. She leaned forward clutching her chest. "Something is gripping, pulling, clenching, I can't describe, this, sensation."

Garrett looked around the chamber. He saw no figure, silhouette, shadow, or body. He shouted into the air. "Why! Why are you doing this to her? What is our purpose here?"

Silence.

Garrett drew his spear, summoned his aura and manifested his wings. He took flight and circled the room, surveying around and behind the rocks. He soared with the majesty of an eagle, but his eyes resembled those of a vulture, desperate for anything. After three laps around the room, he descended and stood by Anise. She was hunched over, still clasping the light emanating from her chest.

"Hard, to describe," Anise panted and puffed. She winced. Her hand trembled. "Not painful, but somehow, not comfortable either."

"Who are you?" Garrett hollered into the chamber. "What is the purpose of this?"

Silence.

Anise dropped to one knee, then both, chest still illuminating the room. "Can't, sum-mon, aura," she managed.

Garrett knelt beside her. He placed a hand on her hands. The orange light of his aura was drawn to her chest and added a ring of orange around each new pulse of light. Garrett's power coupled with Anise's brightened the cavern beyond daylight.

Garrett looked away, shielding his eyes from the intensity of the light. The light reflected from the glowing red pools, amplifying their light. "What is happening to her?" he demanded of whoever might be listening.

Silence.

Garrett took his hand away from Anise. The orange in her light diminished, leaving only a faint trace.

An unknown voice echoed through the cavern. "The pulses of light are less intense feeding from a trace instead of using Garrett's aura directly."

"Who's there?" Garrett shouted, spinning to find the source. "Identify yourself, then slowly advance and be recognized." He kept his spear pointed forward, ready to lunge.

"Put down the toy," the voice replied coyly. "I'm simply here to talk."

"Show yourself then," Garrett insisted, spear at the ready.

A tendril of purple light blinked across the room and wrapped around Garrett.

"If I wanted you dead, you would be dead," the voice said with smug certainty. "You're currently alive because you protected my daughter?"

"Daughter?" Anise gasped. "Mother? Are you, my mother?"

"I am, child," the voice replied. "I am Lilith, mother of all demons, and you, sweet you, are the product of centuries of work. Now, the time has come."

"Centuries? Work? Time has come?" Anise repeated. Her eyes blinked and she grabbed her chest. She rotated her neck, looking for the body attached to the voice. Anise was frozen from the shoulders down.

"You make her sound like a piece of machinery being refined," Garrett commented.

"You, son of Azazel, were not expressly invited," Lilith's voice snapped. "Your presence here is simply to assist my daughter in understanding. Keep your place."

Garrett stood silent. Anise was a statue. Her hand dropped to her side. The light from her chest changed from a pulse to a constant glow. "Mother, what are you saying?"

A woman emerged from behind stalagmites at one end of the cavern. She was tall and slender with long black hair. Her black clothing with purple accents hugged her curvy body. Curved horns extended from the top of her head. Black bat wings reached from her shoulders to her ankles. "Daughter, you have suffered a long time. Be assured there is a reward for the trials you endured."

Anise stared Lilith in the eyes. "What reward does a life of suffering bring? Scars? Fears? Distrust of others?"

"I see from the silver light you've discovered the secret you carry," Lilith said.

"Secret?" Garrett asked.

"Don't feign ignorance," Lilith hissed. "You are both aware of her angelic bloodline and the latent power it carries."

Garrett stood silently. His grip on his spear remained firm.

"How is this even possible?" Anise asked. "How am I an angel and a demon?"

"I bred with a Celestial who hadn't realized his powers," Lilith answered. "As queen of the succubi, mother of demons, the seductress I am, he was unable to refuse my advances. The result was an Infernal son."

"A son?" Anise questioned.

"Your great great grandfather," Lilith replied. "I wanted a latent trace of angelic power in a child with a higher proportion of demonic power," Lilith continued. "I bore another child, sired by that son. Then I bore another and another. Finally, I bore you."

"That, that's four generations," Anise commented. "You said centuries."

"Infernals can live longer than normal mortals," Lilith said. "Your demon blood should double your lifespan, maybe even triple it. I waited for the children of my experiment to age so their abilities, even if unawakened, were surely present."

Anise stared blankly. "Does this mean you're my mother, grandmother, and great-grandmother?"

"Yes, child," Lilith replied. "That may be difficult for your human mind to comprehend. It's best we move forward and not dwell on such things."

"That seems unimaginable," Garrett commented.

"Incest is a concern reserved for humans," Lilith replied with a sly wink. "Anise was bred for a purpose. Strong sires were needed, as was a strong mother."

"You make it sound like breeding horses," Garrett said. "A strong mare paired with a champion stallion."

"In her case, it was a strong stallion and a champion mare," Lilith chuckled.

"Why have I been summoned now?" Anise asked. "Why not when I awakened, or when I was a child, to be raised under your guidance?"

"You were needed as you are now," Lilith replied, circling the room and assessing Anise from head to toe.

"As I am now?"

"Yes, Anise," Lilith answered. "Now you are aware of your angelic power. You manifested angelic power and have the ability to access the divine energy."

"Why was she needed like that?" Garrett demanded.

Lilith's tail sailed through the air and lashed Garrett across the face. His hand instinctively covered his cheek and his spear dropped to the ground. He let out a muffled cry.

"I told you to keep your place," Lilith hissed. "I dislike repeating myself."

Garrett's face scrunched. His lips opened, exposing his grinding teeth.

"Your anger is refreshing," Lilith chuckled. "Your restraint is impressive. Many have tried to attack after receiving that lash; it never ends well for them."

"Mother," Anise said. "Why am I needed as I am now? I do not fully understand."

"Child," Lilith began. "Sweet child, you were bred to be a bridge; a way to combine the angelic and the demonic in one vessel."

"You continue to make it sound like horse breeding, now combined with some twisted alchemy or science experiment," Anise replied.

"You're to be a tool of war, my child," Lilith responded.

"A tool of war?" Anise repeated, her eyes stricken with terror.

"As with many of my children," Lilith explained, "I breed demons for the purpose of battling to return home to the heavens."

"Home?" Anise asked. "I was always taught that hell was the home of devils and demons."

Lilith cackled with glee. "Oh Anise, if they only told you the truth. Your religious leaders focus on their concept of good and evil too much. I was the first woman. I was meant to be the mother to all. Lucifer was an angel, one of the brightest. Azazel, Beliel, Asmodeus, Beelzebub, Mephistopheles, myself, we all sought what the humans had but we did not, the capacity to grow and develop beyond that which we were created to be. For this, we were labelled rebellious and cast out. Our only course to return to the beauty we once called home is by force."

"And there are those who would thwart your efforts," Garrett commented.

Lilith replied by slapping him across the chest with her tail. He stumbled backwards four steps before regaining his balance.

Silence.

Anise broke the silence. "I still don't understand how I can only be of use with angelic power."

"Being an angel, there are barriers you can pass through, child," Lilith answered. "That is the key which will unlock the gate."

"One succubus seems absurdly small for an advance force," Garrett said.

Lilith ignored him.

"He's correct," Anise said. "I can't battle the entire might of Heaven alone. No Infernal, no demon, could even accomplish that task."

"Sweet Anise," Lilith chuckled. "Your innocence knows no limits." Lilith strolled up to Anise with a smile on her face. She ran a finger from Anise's ear to chin, then cupped Anise's chin. "This face is still so young. So much in your life, and yet still so far to grow."

"Far to grow?" Anise scoffed. "I'm an adult."

Lilith cackled with glee. "In the eyes of man, you are grown. In the eyes of a greater demon with tens of thousands of children who have lived for millennia, you, my most recent child, are still just a baby."

"And how far do I have to grow to be a match for the forces of Heaven?" Anise asked. "How do I breach the gates and survive?"

"That's why you were summoned," Lilith replied, maintaining her sinister grin.

Anise frowned slightly, then puffed her lips to pout. "You make it sound like I was summoned prematurely. Why summon me for a mission I'm admittedly unfit to even consider?"

"Summoning," Lilith exclaimed opening her arms in front of her. "You pass the gates, and then you summon a legion of demons."

"I don't know how to summon," Anise replied.

Lilith smiled. "Ah, but you will." She started walking toward an opening in the cavern wall. Her arm extended and her finger curled in beckoning Anise. "Follow me."

Anise and Garrett followed a few paces behind Lilith. As they passed through the doorway, they saw an altar table with a massive red glowing rock.

"It feels so familiar," Garrett said.

"This is the Patron Stone," Lilith said. "It has the ability to bestow unimaginable power on whomever it sees fit."

"Does it consider us fit?" Anise asked.

"For the task at hand you are the most qualified," Lilith laughed. "No other demon has Celestial blood."

"This is so much to comprehend all at once," Anise whispered. "Will I truly be capable of such a monumental feat?"

"Come, my child," a voice said. It was the same voice which had taken over Aleesa.

"Who are you?" Anise asked.

"I am the stone," the voice replied. "Come closer."

Anise crept toward the stone. Garrett walked up behind her. He placed his hand on her shoulder. "We will face this together."

During their approach, Anise's stone fragment glowed brighter and brighter. The two stones vibrated and made a high-pitched squeal. They stopped mere inches from the altar. The stone's radiance was blinding in the otherwise dim cavern.

"Place your hand on me," the stone insisted.

Anise stood motionless. "Why do you require contact? Shouldn't I be able to channel this power?"

Lilith appeared behind Anise and whispered over her shoulder. "The DHEC energy you channel is a mere flicker of the true raging fire the stone possesses. Direct exposure has comparatively unimaginable effects."

"Will I lose myself to this power?" Anise asked.

"No, Anise," Lilith replied quickly. "You will not be lost. You will be evolved; elevated beyond the abilities of even the greatest Infernals. You will rank just below the greater demons. Imagine it. You will have that kind of ability, the power to stop the Touched, the power to mark and seal humanity to our cause."

"The Touched," Anise said with a grin. "I wish I'd never heard that word."

"What do you mean?" Garrett asked.

A tear rolled down Anise's cheek. "Since I awakened, so much has happened. I've been trying to understand this new world and how I'm affected by it. Now I have to change again. I have new powers, new rules, a new role to play. How many times will that change again? How many will I need to kill? How much suffering will I cause?"

"You're a demon, child," Lilith whispered with a slight hiss. "Demons kill, demons cause suffering. Your role, slayer of those abominations, kills a source of grief and suffering. You're a demon, but also a saviour."

"After they're saved and marked the humans are bound to an eternity in Hell," Anise retorted. "I simply trade one suffering for another for our benefit. That hardly seems like the act of a saviour."

"Don't the Celestials do the same?" Lilith snapped. Her eyes focused on Anise, glaring, burning, right down to her core. "They save people. They consecrate a bond. They bring souls to their camp. They fuel their armies in the same manner we do."

The cavern shook. "ENOUGH!" the stone boomed.

Garrett and Anise jumped. Lilith backed away from Anise slightly.

"Come, Anise, touch me," the stone ordered.

Anise looked at Garrett, then to Lilith, at the stone, and then met eyes with Garrett again. Her eyes full of concern, a tremble in her voice, she whispered to Garrett, "I'm scared."

Garrett nodded. "We both are. Not even in our wildest dreams could we ever have imagined standing here."

"Hurry," Lilith whispered. "Become strong. Strong so you can stop the Touched. Strong so you can defeat those Celestials who stood by as you suffered through life. Strong so you can lead the charge."

"Touch me!" the stone demanded, "or the man dies."

A tendril of red smoke wafted from the stone and wrapped around Garrett. The tendril sprouted others. They wrapped Garrett's arms, legs, and neck. The smoke tightened. It pulled Garrett's arms and legs spreadeagle. The smoke coiled around his neck, once, twice, a third coil crept over his mouth and nose.

Garrett coughed. "Hard to breathe. Can't move. Can't summon my aura."

"STOP!" Anise shouted.

"Come to me," the stone demanded.

Anise crept the last few steps to reach the stone. She cautiously extended her arm. The smoke relaxed around Garrett and he gasped for air. Anise's fingers brushed the stone. Her eyes and mouth quivered. Her aura glowed. The stone's aura and Anise's swirled together at each of her fingertips.

"Ah-ah, what is this feeling?" Anise asked.

The stone released Garrett. The smoke began to swirl around Anise. "This is the power I can bestow upon you," came the reply.

The smoke swirling around Anise focused itself in front of her chest. Her fragment of the stone glowed. The smoke focused itself and compressed to the width of a finger. The stone on the altar pulsed and shrank, pebbles floated in the aura. The pebbles mingled, flowing through the aura, toward Anise, into her chest, traces of pebble-free aura wafted up and entered her mouth.

"What's happening?" Garrett gasped.

"The stone is merging with her," Lilith replied. "This is what they were both nurtured for."

"Nurtured?" Garrett repeated.

"Yes," Lilith said. "The stone was nurtured by all the demonic energy that flowed through it. Everything from greater demons to lesser demons of all kinds and Infernals. The stone has withheld bits of energy every time some passed through."

"What about Anise?" Garrett asked. "From what I've seen nothing was ever done to nurture her."

"She was raised to be the vessel," Lilith said. "A vessel of both demonic and angelic power. A vessel with no emotional ties. A vessel that understands pain and inflicts justice in the name of those wronged."

"What justice?" Garrett asked. "Who was wronged? I don't understand."

"Clearly," Lilith chuckled. "Anise grew up seeing prostitutes mistreated. She was mistreated herself as an orphan. She grew up to dispense her own brand of justice on those who would do wrong to women like her."

"Someone taught her about drugs," Garrett stated. "That's not nurturing. Random acts aren't the same as growing up with love or parents."

Lilith scoffed. "What would an orphaned fury spawn know of family or parents?"

Garrett's teeth clenched then loosened. "I found a man to call brother. I saw other children with their families. I know what we missed. No parents to care for or teach us…"

"I taught her!" Lilith shouted. "I was there, in disguise, affecting her memory so she would develop on her own. Of all my daughters she is among the most important."

"Are you serious!" Anise shouted. "You trained me. You watched me. You did nothing either. And you try to vilify the Celestials for standing idly by as I suffered. You caused my suffering? You were the driving force. How dare you?"

Lilith stepped back. Her wings extended, fully open. Her tail started whipping wildly behind her. "You dare speak to me that way?"

The stone was little more than a pebble. The aura and smoky energy swirled around Anise. She summoned her aura and wings. One bat wing and one feathered wing appeared. The aura surrounding Anise had traces of silver, purple, and crimson intertwined. Her aura whip crackled as it manifested from her hand. Anise sprouted a tail matching Lilith's.

"Daughter," Lilith laughed. "You've progressed nicely. Can you feel the energy flowing through you? Are you prepared to learn the technique for summoning demons?"

"No," Anise replied. "I have no intention of being a puppet."

Lilith glared at her. "Child, you are no match for me, and he certainly isn't." Lilith shifted her gaze toward Garrett. Her devious smile combined sly and sinister. "You don't want him to die, do you?"

Lilith's tail sprang forward and wrapped around Garrett's throat. Anise extended her arm. Her aura flowed to Garrett's hand. Garrett's aura manifested. The orange glow and black feathered wings flashed out from his body. The aura around his neck fought the grip from Lilith's tail.

"He struggles against my tail," Lilith observed. "What will happen if I unveil my true strength?"

Garrett's spear retracted. His orange aura sword shot forward and extended to Lilith's chest. The attack was stopped by Lilith's aura.

"Child's play," she cackled dismissively. "You couldn't break through in a thousand years. Let me show you some of my strength."

Lilith tightened the grip her tail had around Garrett's throat. The tail dug through his aura, squeezing it out. Garrett began to gasp for air.

Anise flicked her wrist and slapped Lilith's face with her aura whip. Lilith's head instinctively turned at the moment of impact and her cheek started to darken in colour.

"He may be just an Infernal," Anise said, "but I'm supposed to be strong enough to enter Heaven and be the advance force on my own."

Anise flicked her whip and tail toward Lilith. She channelled the tri-coloured aura through both. Lilith recoiled from each strike but maintained her grasp on Garrett. Anise adjusted her attacks, focusing on beating at the base of Lilith's tail.

"You may be stronger than he is," Lilith said. "You're still millennia away from reaching my level."

Lilith manifested a crackling purple and black whip. She flicked it out toward Garrett. He managed to move his aura sword to intercept. Lilith's whip wrapped around Garrett's sword. They both fought for control. While they struggled, Anise whipped Lilith across the hand. The momentary lapse from Lilith dismissed her whip. Once the hold was broken Garrett almost fell backward tugging on his sword. Lilith's tail loosened around Garrett's neck as his aura pressed it back.

"You can stall," Lilith hissed, "but you cannot emerge victorious."

Lilith released Garrett. She drew a sword and ran her aura through it. Lilith pointed the sword at Anise. The aura shot forward creating a line of crackling purple and black energy. Anise lashed at the aura blade with her aura whip. Lilith used her tail to intercept. Anise tried her own tail. Lilith blocked that using a whip made of aura. Anise drew her dagger. Lilith thrust her arm forward, her aura blade sped up. Anise was able to deflect the aura blade away from her heart but was impaled through the shoulder.

Garrett lunged toward Lilith. He pierced her abdomen with his aura sword. Lilith howled in pain. Ichor oozed from the wound.

"How is this possible?" Lilith roared holding the wound and inspecting the ichor.

Anise laughed while holding her shoulder. "I have the stone in me. I knew you'd ignore Garrett's attack and focus on me, so I channelled a huge amount of DHEC energy into Garrett."

"A desperate maneuver," Lilith remarked. "Acts of self-sacrifice have one huge flaw though. If they don't work, you run out of sacrifices quickly."

Garrett lunged for Lilith again. She caught his aura sword with her aura whip. Garrett struggled but Lilith held firm as she walked toward Anise.

Anise's blood soaked her dress. The spot grew into a fist-sized blob and continued to expand. She panted heavily and her eyes squinted.

Lilith approached Anise, sword in hand, black and purple aura crackling in the otherwise dark and silent cavern. "If you refuse to accept your destiny, I'll just have to kill you and start over."

Garrett roared. He dismissed his aura sword and extended his spear. The orange crackle returned, free of Lilith's whip. Garrett took flight. He strafed past Lilith, barely managing to poke her. Lilith laughed. Garrett swooped around for another pass. He jabbed and struck Lilith's wing.

Lilith shrieked as the spear punched a hole in her wing membrane. Garrett retracted his spear back to handle size, then extended it for his next run.

Panting, struggling to stand, Anise dropped to one knee. With one hand on her wound, she channelled aura to the other and formed a whip. She used the whip to strike at Lilith's injured wing. Lilith intercepted with her tail. Anise sent her own tail after Lilith. It wrapped around her leg. Anise fell backward. Lilith stumbled forward, arms and wings out and fluttering for balance. Garrett saw the opening. He soared in and plunged his spear into Lilith's back.

Lilith roared as Garrett stopped in midair and twisted the spear. He jerked and jabbed at the handle. The head of the spear dug into Lilith's flesh. Ichor oozed out and flowed down her back and legs.

Lilith howled out a deafening scream. As the waves of sound rippled out from her body, they carried currents of Lilith's aura. As each crashed into Anise and Garrett they recoiled as though physically struck.

"What is this?" Garrett called out.

The shriek continued. Garrett was forced to land and retract his wings. Anise went from one knee to crumpled in a ball on the cavern floor.

Lilith swung her arm. An aura whip flew forth and slapped Garrett across the face. He fell to the ground.

"Garrett!" Anise yelled.

He didn't move.

"GARRETT!" Anise screamed.

Lilith cackled. "I doubt he can hear, or help you now."

"You, you monster," Anise panted out. "How could you."

Lilith towered over Anise, disdain dripping from her face more than the ichor dripped from her body. "The goals we have are more important than any single life. If you refuse the task assigned, then another will be created. You are the first. I can learn from my mistakes."

"What about, the centuries of waiting?" Anise coughed.

"When you're as old as we are, you'll learn the virtue of patience," Lilith replied. "You, conversely, have no patience, no sense of duty, and now, I'll kill you."

Lilith raised her sword. The black and purple aura formed lightning, bursting and exploding. The sword came down slowly. Lilith measured her executioner's strike. The sword went up.

A blinding white light flashed. When the light faded, Lilith stood in the cavern, alone.

Chapter 21 – Guardians

The flash of light faded. Anise spun around. She stood in white. No shape, no features, surrounded by only white. The cavern, the Patron Stone, Lilith, there was no sign of them.

"Garrett," she called. "Garrett, can you hear me? Where are we?"

Assessing her surroundings, Anise stood on something white. There was light all around. She couldn't see walls or a ceiling of any kind. There was some surface to stand and walk on, smooth and even, but unseen. Anise felt around, hands extended, fingers outstretched reaching for contact with something. No solid objects. She started walking in a growing spiral calling Garrett's name. Eventually, she came across his body laying on the white floor.

"Garrett," she sobbed, placing her hand on his chest. Relief flooded her as she felt his chest rise and fall slightly. Anise's eyes flashed wide open. "A heartbeat, he's alive," she whispered.

Anise stood up and spun in place. She shielded her eyes. "Hello, is anyone here? Where are we? Who are you?"

Anise looked down at her dress. It was soaked in blood. She reached her hand in to check. "Tearing this stuck cloth off could be worse than leaving it," she whispered to herself.

Anise drew her dagger and sat beside Garrett. "Someone brought us here for a purpose," she thought aloud. "They won't stay silent forever. I hope they show themselves before I pass out."

Anise's eyes grew heavy; she leaned into Garrett, part sitting beside part leaning on him. In the white space, she continually scanned. "There's no method of telling time here. How long have we been here? How long until someone approaches us?"

Anise's body slumped against Garrett's, her dagger lay by her side. Her head motions all but stopped. She fought to keep her eyes open. "Who are you?" she called. "Someone show yourself. Why did you bring us here?"

A figure walked out of the light. Anise mouthed her assessment. "An adult, probably male, scabbard at the belt, walking normally so likely uninjured, silhouette doesn't give much other information."

"Anise," a familiar voice called out.

"I recognize your voice, sir, but I'm embarrassed, I must ask to whom does it belong?"

"Alastair," the voice replied. "I've been sent as a messenger."

"Messenger?" Anise repeated. "Sent by whom?"

"Sent by God," Alastair replied. "God wanted me to thank you for absorbing the stone, and for fighting Lilith instead of joining her."

"God knew?" Anise asked.

"God saved you," Alastair replied. "God is all-knowing and all-seeing. Very seldom does a direct intervention happen." Alastair reached his hand forward. A flow of celestial energy travelled from his fingertips to Anise's shoulder.

Anise watched the energy flow to her wound. "The pain is decreasing," she said. "Thank you. What can you do to help Garrett?"

Alastair extended a second stream of energy. "He was simply knocked unconscious. His wounds will heal in time. You are in more serious need."

Anise sat silently while Alastair used his healing energy. When he finished, she asked, "What happens to us now?"

"I'm here to instruct you," Alastair replied. "The stone you absorbed controls the flow of DHEC energy to both Infernals and Infernal created Touched, like Shamblers and Shifters. If you stop the flow, you stop the Touched."

"How do I stop the flow?" Anise asked.

"Concentrate on the stone in your chest," Alastair said. "Do you feel the flow of energy through you? Do you feel the gates the energy flows through?"

Anise closed her eyes. "It's hard, but I feel some of them." She paused. "Now more. My goodness, there are so many."

"Visualize the entry and exit points as doors," Alastair instructed. "Then, shut the doors. You may need to shut them one at a time due to fatigue."

Anise opened her eyes. "What about Celestials and Celestial created Touched?"

"Once the war on Earth is stopped from the demon side, God will close the gates of heavenly energy. There is no need for soldiers when there is no opponent or battlefield."

"Then what happens?" Anise asked.

"Mortal life resumes as it did without otherworldly intrusions," Alastair answered.

"What about Garrett? He was labelled a deserter. He would be put to death if caught."

"The memories and interactions regarding Infernals and Celestials will be altered," Alastair replied. "For everyone else, it will be as though life carried on as normal. Garrett will return to the guard with a promotion. You will return to your life. The only difference between you and the other humans will be that you will know. You must become the guardian of the stone."

"You mean *we* must," Anise commented. "When fighting Lilith, I transferred some of the stone into Garrett. While I command most, he has an amount of power I cannot close off. We must protect the stone, together."

Alastair's eyes closed. His head cocked up. When his eyes opened, he made eye contact with Anise. "Your request has been approved. You are both to guard the Patron Stone. Your abilities, angelic and demonic, while available, are to be used only in the strictest of secrecy and the most dire of emergencies."

"So, even after all your deception, you want me to join your side of this war?" Anise questioned.

"No," Alastair replied. "Infernals, Celestials, and Touched do not belong in this war. I want you to seal the war away from the human world. God wants you to do this. Accept your angelic side. Become a risen angel."

"I will still control the conduit that is the patron stone?" Anise asked.

"Yes."

"And I still retain the power of the stone and my demonic and angelic properties?"

"Yes."

"You're simply requesting I put an end to human suffering at the hands of the Touched?"

"That's correct," Alastair confirmed.

"What assurance do I have you'll keep your word?" Anise asked.

"Currently, I act as a messenger for God. There can be no higher assurance than the word of God."

"You saved Garrett for me," Anise said. "I should try to trust you and help mankind."

"Excellent!" Alastair proclaimed. "I'll have you wake in your home."

"Pardon m....." Anise couldn't finish the question before a flash of light interrupted.

■ ■

Anise awoke, sitting slowly. She noticed a body laying on the bed beside her. Her body tensed. Her eyes bulging, lip quivering, hands shaking, she lifted the blanket. Anise breathed a sigh of relief. "Still clothed."

Anise climbed out of bed. It was nice and comfortable, feathers perhaps, not rough straw. She crept around to see the face of the man. It was Garrett. She breathed a sigh of relief. Exploring the room, Anise found a wardrobe. Guard uniforms on one side, nice dresses on the other, nightshirts for both she and Garrett in the middle, drawers with socks and stockings.

She ventured out of the bedroom. It looked like the abandoned house they stayed in, but not abandoned. There was a dining table, chairs, a woodpile beside the hearth, oil lamps on end tables, and a modest couch.

"It looks so different," Anise said. "Is this truly my life now?"

She opened the pantry. "Flour, sugar, potatoes, onions, jars of preserves, apples, carrots, this is so much."

She spun around at the sound of a creaking noise. It was coming from the bedroom. Garrett wandered out into the main room. "Anise? What happened? Where are we?"

Anise walked to the couch and beckoned Garrett to sit with her. "Sit, Garrett. You were unconscious for a while. We have a few items to discuss."